'It's no use guessing,' declared Biggles. 'No doubt he'll tell
us how it happened when he arrives — not that it
matters very much now. Von Stalhein has got us in a
nasty jam, and it would be foolish to deny it. Still, it
isn't the first time.'

# BIGGLES BOOKS
# PUBLISHED IN THIS EDITION

FIRST WORLD WAR:
Biggles Learns to Fly
Biggles Flies East
Biggles the Camels are Coming
Biggles of the Fighter Squadron

SECOND WORLD WAR:
Biggles Defies the Swastika
Biggles Delivers the Goods
Biggles Defends the Desert
Biggles Fails to Return

# BIGGLES
## DEFIES *the*
### SWASTIKA

## CAPTAIN W.E. JOHNS

**RED FOX**

Red Fox would like to express their grateful thanks
for help given in the preparation of these editions to Jennifer Schofield,
author of *By Jove, Biggles*, Linda Shaughnessy of A. P. Watt Ltd
and especially to the late John Trendler.

BIGGLES DEFIES THE SWASTIKA
A RED FOX BOOK 0 09 947735 1

First published in Great Britain by Oxford University Press 1941

This Red Fox edition published 2003

3 5 7 9 10 8 6 4 2

Papers used by Random House Children's Books are natural, recyclable products
made from wood grown in sustainable forests. The manufacturing processes
conform to the environmental regulations of the country of origin.

Red Fox Books are published by Random House Children's Books,
61–63 Uxbridge Road, London W5 5SA,
a division of The Random House Group Ltd,
in Australia by Random House Australia (Pty) Ltd,
20 Alfred Street, Milsons Point, Sydney, NSW 2061, Australia,
in New Zealand by Random House New Zealand Ltd,
18 Poland Road, Glenfield, Auckland 10, New Zealand,
and in South Africa by Random House (Pty) Ltd,
Endulini, 5A Jubilee Road, Parktown 2193, South Africa

THE RANDOM HOUSE GROUP Limited Reg. No. 954009

A CIP catalogue record for this book is available from the British Library.

Printed and bound in Great Britain by
Cox & Wyman Ltd, Reading, Berkshire

# Contents

# Chapter 1

# An Unpleasant Awakening

Squadron-Leader James Bigglesworth, D.S.O., better known in flying circles as 'Biggles', was awakened by the early morning sun streaming through the open window of his room in the Hotel Kapital, in Oslo. As he stretched out his hand towards the bedside bell, to let the chambermaid know that he was ready for his coffee, he became vaguely aware that instead of the usual bustle in the street below there was a peculiar silence, as if it were Sunday. It struck him that he might be mistaken in the day, and that it was Sunday after all; but this thought was instantly dismissed by the absence of church-bell chimes. He reached out for the morning paper, which the hall porter, without wakening him, had on previous days put on his bedside table, only to frown with surprise and disapproval when he found that it was not there.

Looking back, he could never understand why this sequence of events did not suggest the truth to him. Perhaps he was not fully awake; or it may have been that his mind was filled with other things. Be that as it may, no suspicion of the real state of affairs occurred to him. He was in no immediate hurry to get up, for he had nothing in particular to do, so he lay still, basking in the early spring sunshine, thinking over the peculiar nature of the mission that had brought him to Norway, and wondering if it was time for him to get into touch with Colonel Raymond, of the British Intelligence Service, with a view to asking if he could now return to France.

When, some two months earlier, Colonel Raymond had broached the project to him, Biggles had listened without enthusiasm, for he was quite content to be where he was. At that time he was in France, commanding a special squadron which included amongst its pilots his two best friends, Flight-Lieutenant the Hon. Algy Lacey and Flying-Officer 'Ginger' Hebblethwaite; and one of the reasons why he received Colonel Raymond's proposal with disfavour was that the acceptance of it meant leaving them, and going alone to Norway.

The mission which Colonel Raymond asked him to undertake was, on the face of it, neither difficult nor dangerous. Briefly, it was this. According to reports received from their secret agents, the British authorities were of the opinion that the Nazi government contemplated an invasion of Scandinavia, and in the event of this taking place, British troops would at once be sent to the assistance of the country attacked. But this was only the major issue. If troops were sent, then they would have to be supported by aircraft, and Colonel Raymond's department was anxious to ascertain what air bases would be available. This did not mean established civil or military aerodromes, particulars of which were already known, but tracts of land which might, in emergency, be converted into aerodromes. Failing that, which lakes or fiords were the most suitable for marine aircraft? Such technical information as this could only be obtained by a practical pilot, and Biggles was asked to undertake the work. There were, however, minor difficulties, one of which was the political aspect. For example, if it became known that a British pilot was carrying out survey flights over Norway it might lead to unpleasant repercussions, and in order to avoid such a possibility a scheme had been evolved.

Biggles — assuming that he accepted the task — would proceed to Norway as a Norwegian subject who had for many years resided in Canada. This would account for his being able to speak English fluently, and at the same time explain his imperfect Norwegian. As a matter of fact, Biggles knew no Norwegian at all, and his first job would be to pick up the language as quickly as possible. For the rest, he would be provided with papers pronouncing him to be Sven Hendrik, born in Oslo. On arriving in Norway he would join a flying club and buy a light aeroplane in which he would make cross-country flights, ostensibly for sport, but in reality to collect the information required. Should the threatened invasion actually occur, all he would have to do would be to get into his machine and fly back to England forthwith.

It all sounded so very simple that it found no favour in Biggles's eyes, and he said as much, pointing out that it was a job any pilot could do. But Colonel Raymond, with shrewd foresight, did not agree. He admitted that while all went well the mission was unlikely to present any difficulty, but should unforeseen circumstances arise — well, it would save him a lot of anxiety if someone of ability and experience was on the job. It would not last very long — perhaps two to three months. If he, Biggles, would undertake it, Algy Lacey could command the squadron in France until he returned.

In the end Biggles had agreed to go, for as the matter

was put to him he could not very well refuse, particularly as Colonel Raymond asked him to go as a personal favour. So he said good-bye to Algy and Ginger and in due course arrived in Norway. He would, of course, have taken his two comrades with him had this been possible, but Colonel Raymond vetoed it on the grounds that three strangers might attract suspicion where one would not.

For nearly two months he had been in Norway, making long survey flights in his little 'Moth' when the weather permitted, and swotting hard at the Norwegian language on every possible occasion. To live in a country is the best and quickest way of learning its language, and after seven weeks of concentrated effort Biggles was able to carry on a normal conversation in Norwegian. Also, by flying over it, he had got to know the country very well; indeed, there were few physical features that he had not seen, including the rugged coast-line. He had sent his reports home with many photographs, so it was reasonable to suppose that he might be recalled at any moment. Indeed, it was in anticipation of this that he had left his room at the flying club, which was a small private landing-ground near the village of Boda, to see the sights. Oslo was only thirty miles from Boda. He apprehended no danger in leaving his base, for nothing of note had happened the whole time he had been in Norway, and as far as he could see nothing was likely to happen. In fact, in his heart he was beginning to suspect that the British Intelligence Service had been mistaken in thinking that the Germans were contemplating an attack on Norway.

He looked at his watch. It was now nearly eight o'clock, and still his coffee had not arrived. This was curious, for the chambermaid was usually prompt, and he was in the act of reaching again for the bell when a sound reached his ears that brought a puzzled frown to his forehead. However, still without alarm, he flung off the bedclothes and was on his way to the window when the door of the room burst open and the chambermaid appeared. She seemed to be in a state of bordering on hysteria.

'What's the matter?' asked Biggles shortly.

The woman nearly choked in her excitement and dismay. With a quivering finger she pointed to the window. 'The Germans,' she gasped. 'The Germans are here!'

Biggles experienced an unpleasant shock, for he realized that the woman was speaking the truth. Two swift strides took him to the window. One glance was enough. A double file of Nazi troops were marching up the street. A few civilians stood on the pavement watching with expressions that revealed what they felt, but otherwise the street was comparatively deserted.

Biggles bustled the woman out of the room. He had often found it necessary to dress quickly, but never before had he got into his clothes with such speed as he did now. And all the time his brain was racing as he strove to form a plan, to make some provision for the alarming contingency that had arisen; in other words, to escape with all possible speed from the trap in which he found himself.

Where the Nazi troops had come from so miraculously, and apparently without opposition, he could not imagine. At least, he assumed that there had been no opposition, or he could not have failed to hear the firing. The thing was inexplicable. The Nazis, incontestably, were in control of the city, and that was sufficient reason for him to evacuate it with all possible speed. Curiously enough he did not expect any great difficulty in achieving this, for was he not, to all intents and purposes, a harmless Norwegian citizen? Even the Nazis, he reasoned, would hardly massacre the entire civil population in cold blood, nor would they prevent people from going about their normal business.

Before he had finished dressing Biggles had decided on his line of action. It was the obvious one. He would charter a taxi and drive straight to the aerodrome. Once there it would not take him long to get his machine out of its hangar and into the air; and once in the air, only engine failure would prevent him from reaching England. Fortunately, from sheer habit, he had seen his tanks filled before he left the aerodrome. So, broadly speaking, his flight—in both senses of the word—seemed a fairly simple matter. His luggage didn't matter; there was nothing incriminating in it, and nothing that was irreplaceable, so he was quite prepared to abandon it. His only thought was to get to the aerodrome.

He took a quick glance at himself in the full-length mirror and decided that there was no reason why anyone should suspect that he was anything but what he pretended to be—a Norwegian subject. His grey flannel suit he had actually bought in Oslo on his arrival in the country. His nationality papers were in order and he had plenty of ready money, so it seemed that he had little to worry about. Humming nonchalantly, he went down the stairs into the hall, and there he received his first shock. It was a rude one.

Four German troopers, under an *unteroffizier*,* were there. They saw him at the same moment that he saw them, and as to retire would obviously invite suspicion he kept on his way. He was brought to a halt by the point of a bayonet. The *unteroffizier* addressed him harshly.

'Who are you?' he barked.

Biggles affected an expression of surprise. 'My name's Hendrik,' he answered at once. 'Why do you ask? What is happening here?'

'Norway is now under the control of the Third Reich,' answered the German. 'Return to your room and remain there until further notice.'

Biggles looked at the hotel manager. Slumped in his desk, he was as white as death. He seemed stunned. 'It is correct,' he said in a low voice.

Biggles shrugged his shoulders. 'Very well,' he said, and walked back up the stairs.

But this state of affairs did not suit him. Far from it. The last thing he intended doing was to sit passively in his room, so as soon as he was on the first floor he hurried to the end of the corridor and looked out of the window. It overlooked a courtyard—full of Germans. Plainly, there was no escape that way. He tried the windows of several unoccupied rooms, and finally found one overlooking a narrow side street. The only people in it were a small group of women, talking excitedly. They were, of course, Norwegians, so having nothing to fear from them, he opened the window wide, climbed over the sill, and, after hanging to the full extent of his arms, dropped lightly to the pavement. Another moment and he was walking briskly down the

* German: Non-commissioned officer e.g a Sergeant or Corporal.

street towards a garage which he had previously noted. But alas for his hopes! A squad of Germans had already taken possession of the building, so Biggles walked on without pausing.

He was now somewhat at a loss, for although he had been in Oslo twice before, he was by no means sure of his way. He reached the main street to find it full of marching Germans, with Norwegians standing about watching them helplessly. What upset him, however, was the complete absence of motor traffic, and he realized with something like dismay that the invaders must have at once put a ban on mechanical transport. This was disturbing to say the least of it, but it did not affect his determination to get to the aerodrome. Nevertheless, he knew it was no use thinking of walking; it would take too long. He perceived that if the Germans had stopped motor traffic they would also have stopped private flying—or they would as soon as they reached the aerodrome. Thus, his only chance in getting away lay in reaching the aerodrome before the German troops took it over—as they certainly would.

He was standing at the edge of the kerb wondering which way to go when an errand-boy dismounted from a bicycle not far away, and, leaving the machine leaning against a lamp-post, disappeared into a shop. Covertly watching the people around him to see if his movements were observed, Biggles walked quickly to the cycle. Nobody took the slightest notice of him; they were all far too interested in the Germans. In a moment he had straddled the machine and was pedalling a somewhat erratic course down the street—erratic because it was many years since he had ridden a bicycle. Moreover, the only bicycles he had ridden were the rather heavy old-fashioned type which had upright frames, whereas his present mount was a light roadster with ram's-horn handlebars that swept nearly to the ground. He felt awkward on it, clumsy, and could only hope that he did not look as conspicuous as he felt.

Even so, it was entirely the German's fault that he collided with him. He—Biggles—was just turning into the broad highway which he knew ran past the aerodrome when the Nazi, a corporal, stepped right in front of him. Biggles did his best to stop, but he couldn't find the brake, and the result was that the handlebars caught the German under the seat of his pants and knocked him flying into the gutter.

Biggles stopped at once, for he knew that to go on was to court disaster. The corporal, white with fury—for several of the spectators had laughed at his discomfiture—strode swiftly back to where Biggles was standing.

'Fool!' he snarled, kicking the bicycle out of the way and striking Biggles across the face with his open palm.

By what effort Biggles controlled himself he did not know. He clenched his fists and his jaws clamped together, but he stood still, suffering in impotent silence, for around him were a dozen or more fully armed soldiers. But even now the corporal was not satisfied. He lifted his heavy field boot to kick. Biggles stiffened, and his eyes glinted dangerously, for to stand still and be kicked by a German corporal was more than he was prepared to endure. How the matter would have ended had there not been an interruption is a matter for conjecture, but at that moment a Storm-troop* officer on a swastika-bedecked motor-cycle

* A member of an elite force of highly trained troops.

pulled up alongside and spoke crisply to the corporal, demanding to know why he wasn't getting on with his job. Without waiting for the corporal to answer he fired out a string of orders.

The corporal saluted, mustered his men, and marched them behind the officer to the corner of the street, a distance of perhaps forty paces, where the officer proceeded to post the men as sentries.

Biggles looked at his bicycle. The front wheel was buckled and the tire was flat. Obviously, it would take him no farther. There was not another vehicle in sight—except the Nazi-flagged motor-cycle, resting on its stand as the officer had left it.

It did not take Biggles long to make up his mind what to do. He knew now that once the German net had closed around the city he would be caught in it, and would probably remain in it until the end of the war—if nothing worse happened to him. His only chance of escape lay in reaching the aerodrome immediately. In an hour, two hours at most, it would be too late. The motor-cycle offered a chance, a chance that might never present itself again. Biggles had spent most of his life taking chances, and he did not hesitate to take this one.

There was a gasp of horror from the spectators as he swung a leg over the saddle. His heel slammed down the self-starter. There was a yell from the Germans as the engine sprang to life, but he did not waste valuable time looking back. In a moment he was tearing down the street, crouching low over the handlebars to minimize the risk of being hit by the shots which he presumed would follow.

16

# Chapter 2
# Alarming Developments

Actually, only two or three shots were fired, and they whistled harmlessly past, before Biggles came to a side street into which he lost no time in turning. Then he steadied his pace, for he did not want another collision, nor did he wish to attract attention to himself by riding at a dangerous speed. A hundred yards farther on he took a turning which brought him back to the main road. Several parties of German troops were stationed at various turnings and cross-roads, and although they sometimes looked at him curiously as he swept past, they made no attempt to stop him. He realized that he, a civilian, must have cut a strange figure on a swastika-flagged motor-cycle, but the Nazi emblem acted as a passport, and he was content to let the flags remain.

In five minutes he was through the suburbs of the city and on the open road, doing sixty miles an hour, determined that no one should overtake him before he reached the aerodrome. If there was a pursuit, and he fully expected that there would be one, he saw no sign of it, and when, twenty-five minutes later, he swept into the straight piece of road that led to the aerodrome, he imagined that his escape was assured. He could have shouted with glee as he turned into the short drive that ended at the club-house. He did, in fact, purse his lips to whistle, but the sound died away before it was

17

formed; for outside the club-house was a group of men. One or two were civilians; the rest were in uniform—the grey uniform of the German Air Force.

Shaken though he was by shock, Biggles realized what had happened, and a glance towards the hangars confirmed it. A dozen machines were parked in line—but they were not club aeroplanes. They were Messerschmitts, sleek monoplanes bearing the familiar Latin cross, and the swastika of the German Air Force.

The German pilots, laughing, suddenly spread across the road, raising their arms in salute; and, as Biggles jammed on his brakes and stopped, they crowded round him. One of them, a captain, stepped forward, and Biggles steeled himself for the worst. To his utter and complete amazement the German clapped him on the back with every sign of friendliness.

'Welcome!' he cried.

Biggles's brain seemed to go numb, for not by any stretch of the imagination could he make out what was happening. Far from treating him like an enemy, the Germans seemed pleased to see him. He couldn't understand it at all, and he began seriously to wonder if, after all, the whole thing was not an evil dream. Then, dimly, he began to see daylight—or he thought he did. It was the motor-cycle—or rather, the swastika flags on it. The Germans took him for one of themselves.

But the next remark made by the German captain dispelled this delusion. He took Biggles by the arm in the most friendly manner, although his friendliness had an oily quality which Biggles found it hard to stomach.

'Why didn't you tell us you were one of us?' he said slyly, nudging Biggles with roguish familiarity.

Something in the man's voice made Biggles look at him more closely; and then, for the first time, he recognized him. Doubtless it was the uniform that had so altered him that he had not recognized him at first. He was one of the members of the flying club.

Biggles's brain raced to keep pace with the situation. 'But wouldn't that have been risky?' he said vaguely, in order to gain time. 'I thought you were a Norwegian.'

'So I am,' was the staggering reply, 'but I've always admired the Nazis—and it was made worth my while to play on their side. There were three of us here in the swim, but none of us guessed that you were in it too.'

At last Biggles understood. Three of the members of the flying club were in German pay, and now that he had arrived on a Nazi motor-cycle they assumed, not unnaturally, that he, too, was in Nazi employ. The knowledge shook him to the very core. Spying was something he could understand; there had always been, and always would be, spies. It was one of the oldest professions in the world, and was, after all, a part of the unpleasant business of war. But what he could not understand, and what he could not forgive, was a man playing traitor to his own country. Yet there were three such men here, men who were far worse than spies; they were renegades, traitors in the most despicable sense.

Biggles swallowed something in his throat and forced a sickly smile. 'I wasn't taking any chances,' he said in German. 'As a matter of fact,' he continued, as he saw a new loophole of escape. 'I'm not officially in the German service—yet. I heard a whisper that some of you were, so I bided my time; but as soon as I saw the

19

troops land this morning I borrowed this motor-bike and headed for the aerodrome in the hope of being able to do something.'

'You'll be able to do something,' the other assured him. 'We shall need all the pilots we can get, and having seen something of your flying I can recommend you. Ever flown a Messerschmitt?'

'No.'

'You will, and you'll like it. It's a lovely machine. The trouble will be finding somebody to fight.'

'You don't expect much opposition then?'

The other scoffed. 'None at all. The only military machines in the country are obsolete types.'

'But suppose the British send some machines out?' queried Biggles.

The other laughed scornfully. 'We'll deal with them when they come,' he boasted.

'By the way, is my machine still here?' asked Biggles in a voice which he strove to keep steady. He had no wish to find himself in the German Air Force.

'Yes, but you won't be allowed to fly it. All machines are grounded—the Commandant's orders.'

Biggles nodded. 'Of course—very wise,' he agreed. 'Well, here I am. What ought I to do next?'

'You'll have to wait here until the Commandant arrives, then I'll introduce you to him. No doubt he'll be glad to have you in the service, particularly as you know the country. Here he comes now.'

The man, whose name Biggles now remembered was Kristen, nodded towards a big car that came speeding up the road, a swastika flag fluttering on its bonnet.

Biggles's astute brain had now got the whole situation fairly well straightened out. Kristen, and two other members of the club, had actually got the aerodrome ready for German occupation. A number of Messerschmitts, flown by regular German officers, had already landed. The new Commandant of the station was just arriving to take charge of operations. He, Biggles, was assumed to be of Nazi persuasion, and might, if he played his cards properly, actually be admitted into the German Air Force as a renegade Norwegian. The prospect nauseated him, but he felt that if it offered a chance of escape he would be foolish not to take it. There might even be some satisfaction in beating the Germans at their own underhand game. In any case, he knew that if ever it was learned that he was British he was likely to have a bad time. Should the Germans learn his real name, and the Nazi Intelligence Service hear of his capture, then things would look very black indeed, for they had his record and had good cause to hate him.

The assembled pilots clicked their heels as the Commandant's car came to a stop and he alighted.

'Hauptmann Baron von Leffers,' whispered Kirsten.

There was some delay while the Commandant spoke to the officers, some of whom got into their machines and took off. Von Leffers watched them go and then beckoned to Kristen.

'Good,' he said, 'you have done well. Presently you will be given one of our machines, but before that I want to go over with you the list of all machines and accessories that you have here. You have it prepared?'

'Yes, Herr Kommandant.'

The Baron looked at Biggles. 'Who is this?'

'He is one of us, but as yet his appointment has not been confirmed.'

'So? How is that?'

Kristen explained that Biggles had not been very long in the country and had been flying his own machine. He was, he asserted with more confidence than Biggles' statement warranted, entirely in sympathy with the Nazis, and would like to fly for them.

'You have your own plane?' queried the Commandant.

Biggles bowed German fashion. '*Ja, Herr Kommandant.*'

The Baron smiled drily. 'You must have plenty of money?'

Biggles shrugged. 'I had some, but I have spent most of it. Flying is an expensive pastime.'

'It won't cost you anything now,' returned the Baron. 'I'm afraid we shall have to take your machine. You will be paid for it, of course—after the war.'

'Quite so, Herr Kommandant.'

'And you would like to fly one of our fighters?'

'Yes, Herr Kommandant.'

'Have you any experience of fighting machines?'

'Yes. I was a test pilot for a while in America.'

In making this statement Biggles was telling the truth; for once, in America, he had tested some machines for the British Government with a view to purchase.

'We will see about it,' the Baron promised curtly, and, beckoning to Kristen, walked away.

Biggles was left alone. He was not sorry, for he wanted time to think. He was far from pleased with the situation, but he realized that it might have been worse—a lot worse. He was at least still free, and he only wanted to find himself alone in an aeroplane—

any aeroplane—to make a bee-line for home. It was for this reason, of course, that he had agreed to the suggestion of his flying a German fighter, for a Messerschmitt would suit him just as well as his own machine—better, in fact, since it was both faster and had a longer range. In any case, to dispute the suggestion would at once have made him an object of suspicion. The immediate future was still obscure, but he was prepared to match his wits against those of the Germans.

His chief fear was that he would be followed from Oslo by the fellow whose motor-cycle he had taken, and recognized. And it was for this reason that his first action was to put the machine in a shed out of sight. Then, with the idea of escaping forthwith if it were possible, he made his way to the hangar in which his machine was kept, but a glance showed him that this was now out of the question. The hangar was full of Germans; what was even worse, they had already dismantled all the light aeroplanes to make room for the fighters, and were stacking the components against the end wall. Perceiving that nothing was to be gained by remaining there, particularly as several of the Germans were glancing at him suspiciously, he made his way to what had once been the club-house, but was now the officers' quarters.

As he strolled across, a curious smile played for a moment round the corners of his mouth. His Norwegian 'holiday' seemed to be shaping into something very different.

Presently he encountered Kristen, who, for some reason not altogether apparent, seemed to have taken him under his wing. It appeared that Kristen was one

23

of those fussy, busy people who get satisfaction out of making other people's arrangements for them. Perhaps it flatters their vanity. Anyway, up to a point this suited Biggles quite well, and he played up to the man's weakness. At the moment, no doubt on account of the Nazi invasion and the part he had played in it, Kristen was looking very pleased with himself.

'Have you finished with the Commandant?' inquired Biggles, adopting a meek, almost humble, air. He spoke in German.

'It is useful that you speak German so well.'

Biggles nodded.

'Yes, I've given the Commandant all the information about the place,' went on Kristen. 'Of course, it's unlikely that such a little aerodrome will get as much limelight as the big air bases, but we shall make our mark—you watch it.'

'Yes, I shall certainly watch it,' said Biggles seriously, and he meant it.

'By the way, I've brought you this.' Kristen held out a red armlet bearing a black swastika, within a white circle.

'What's that for?' inquired Biggles.

'To wear. You won't be able to get a uniform until to-morrow, perhaps not for a day or two; in the meanwhile the Commandant says you are to wear this. It will show that you are not an ordinary civilian and may save you trouble with the guards.'

'Thanks.' Biggles took the armlet and fastened it on his sleeve.

'We may as well go and have a bite to eat,' suggested Kristen.

'Good idea,' agreed Biggles, and they walked

together to the officers' mess. He smiled as they went in, for it had been the club dining-room. In a few hours it had been converted into a Nazi military depot. More than once, as he ate the food set before him, Biggles smiled faintly as he wondered what his comrades would think could they see him, swastika on sleeve, calmly eating in a German mess.

Later in the day the Commandant sent for him, and after a close interrogation, in which Biggles's statements were supported by his Norwegian papers of nationality, he was admitted into the German Air Force on probation with the rank of *Leutnant*.\* No uniform was yet available, but the Baron promised to procure one for him in the near future. In the meantime Biggles was to wear the swastika armlet.

Biggles didn't like this; nor did he, in fact, like the whole arrangement, but since refusal to accept the conditions would unquestionably jeopardize his freedom, if not his life, he thought it expedient to accept. He promised himself that it would not be for long.

Indeed, within five minutes of leaving the Commandant's office he was making new plans for flight. He still hoped that it might turn out to be a simple business after all. Heavy gunfire could be heard in the distance, and machines, chiefly Messerschmitts, were constantly coming and going; so he found Kristen and asked him frankly if he could make a flight. The not unnatural retort to this request was, 'Why so soon? What was the hurry?' Biggles answered, reasonably enough, that as he was now in the Air Force but had never flown a Messerschmitt, it was time he put in a bit of practice.

To his disappointment his request was refused, not

\* German rank of Pilot officer

on account of any suspicion on Kristen's part—that was obvious—but because no machines were available for such a purpose. They were all in use.

So Biggles had to make the best of it. He nodded and walked away. His time, he thought, would come. He was rather at a loss to know what to do next, but this, as it turned out, was decided for him—and in no uncertain manner. Rounding a corner of the officers' quarters he came face to face with the officer whose motor-cycle he had borrowed. He had just stepped out of a large touring car in which sat three men wearing the uniform of the dreaded Gestapo.*

* German Nazi secret police

# Chapter 3
# Across The Frontier

Coming face to face as they did they recognized each other instantly, and never did Biggles' presence of mind stand him in greater stead. Before the man could speak, and while his brows were still darkening with anger, Biggles clapped him on the shoulder, laughing at the same time.

'So there you are,' he said cheerfully. 'I was hoping you'd come along. I'm dreadfully sorry for what happened this morning, but I was in the dickens of a mess—and in a hurry. I should have been at the aerodrome the moment our troops arrived, but the fool woman at my hotel forgot to wake me. You were all busy, so rather than worry you I tried to get to the aerodrome by myself. As you saw, I borrowed a bicycle. Then, after the accident, knowing that you'd have no difficulty in getting another machine, I borrowed yours and dashed along here. I would have seen to it that you got it back, of course.'

While he had been speaking, out of the corner of his eye Biggles saw Kristen coming towards him. He now looked at him and cried, 'That's right, isn't it?'

'What is?' asked Kristen, hastening his steps.

'My machine was here.' Biggles didn't say *what* machine.

'Yes, that's right.'

Biggles turned to the Gestapo agent. 'There you are.'

In the face of this evidence the German accepted the explanation, but not with very good grace.

'You'd no right to take my machine,' he growled.

'I admit that,' agreed Biggles readily. 'But don't make a fuss about it, there's a good fellow, or it may lead to trouble for all of us.'

'Where is my motor-cycle now?'

'Here. I put it in the shed for safety. I've reported to the Commandant, so I can now take it back to Oslo if you like.'

'It doesn't matter,' was the gruff reply. 'I've borrowed a car from one of these miserable Norwegians — he won't want it again. The car suits me better than the motor-cycle. Still, you'd better take it back to Oslo some time.'

'Where shall I find you?'

'Leave it in the garage of the Nordic Hotel.'

'Certainly,' Biggles promised. 'Have a glass of beer while you're here? I feel I owe you a drink.'

'No, I haven't time now. I must get back. Naturally, I had to find out who it was who made off with my machine.'

'Of course.'

The German went back to his car, and Biggles drew a deep breath of relief. It had been an awkward moment. Kristen was still standing there, but he announced that he was on his way to the hangars where he had a job to do.

Biggles gave the fellow a dark look as he departed. True, he had been of service to him, but not willingly. Had he known the truth it would have been a different story. As far as Biggles was concerned the man was worse than a spy; he was a traitor, and that was something he could not forgive.

He decided to go over to see if the motor-cycle was still where he had left it. It was, and as he gazed at it a fresh scheme took shape in his mind. It did not make so much appeal to him as his original plan for getting out of the country. But the motor-cycle was, after all, a fast vehicle, and it was not far to the Swedish frontier. Sweden was still a neutral country, and if he could get across the frontier into it there was no reason why he should not assume his real nationality, and tell the truth—that he was a fugitive from the Nazi invasion of Norway. He would report to the nearest British Consul, who could, no doubt, make arrangements for his immediate return home. Thinking it over, Biggles decided that it was a reasonable plan, and decided to put it into operation forthwith.

The sun was now far down in the west, and he reckoned that he had only about half an hour of daylight left; but this did not bother him; indeed, he decided that darkness would probably suit his purpose better than broad daylight. He examined the petrol tank and found that it was nearly full, so as there was nothing to delay him he wheeled the machine out and started the engine. Several Germans were about, but none took any notice of him, and in a few minutes he was cruising down the main road.

It was an anxious journey, for he realized that every man was his enemy. The Norwegians, seeing his Nazi armlet, would hate the sight of him. Any German, were the truth known, would shoot him on sight. Nazis of all ranks were everywhere—in cars, on motor-cycles, in armoured cars, and even light tanks; and Biggles was aghast as, for the first time, he saw how widespread the German movement was. It was obvious that far more Germans had landed than he had at first supposed. He wondered vaguely what the Allies were doing about it all, but of course he had no means of knowing.

The traffic grew more congested as he neared the frontier, chiefly with refugees trying to escape from the country—going anywhere to evade the Nazis. German soldiers and Storm Troopers were turning them back, and from observations made by the people Biggles learned that many of these same Nazis had been living in the country as ordinary citizens, and were known to them. In other words, they had been planted in the country before the invasion actually occurred. Thus Biggles learned of the treachery that enabled the Nazis to effect the landing. Still, his armlet and the swastika-beflagged motor-cycle served their purpose, and took him anywhere he wanted to go. Indeed, on more than one occasion Nazi troops held up the traffic to let him pass.

By this time he had got to within a few miles of the frontier, and the traffic began to thin out. The Germans were fewer, from which he judged that he had about reached the limit of their operations. The calm manner in which peasants were walking home from the fields suggested that they had not yet heard that their country had been invaded.

As twilight closed in and darkness fell, Biggles stopped. A signpost told him that the frontier was only a mile ahead. He contemplated the motor-cycle, and knew that it would not do to try to get into Sweden on such a machine. Already alarmed by what had happened to Norway, the Swedes would not want anything

German in their country. He decided that he would have to abandon the machine, but he hardly liked to leave it by the road-side where it would certainly attract attention, so he turned down a lane and lifted it bodily into the bottom of a deep ditch, near a coppice, covering it with any rubbish he could find so that it would not be noticed by a passer-by. He took off his armlet and pushed it under the saddle.

This done, he made a cautious survey of the landscape, as far as it was possible in the darkness, and then set off at a brisk walk for the frontier. He now had only one fear. Would the Swedes allow a Norwegian to enter the country? For that is what his passport proved him to be—Sven Hendrik, a Norwegian subject. The photograph on the passport, and the particulars it registered, were, of course, correct; only the name was false; but the Swedes, in their natural anxiety, might refuse to allow him to enter the country. Had he possessed any British papers this difficulty would not have arisen; but he had none—it would have been far too dangerous to carry such papers on his person.

As he expected, the frontier barrier was down, but he marched boldly up to it and took his place at the end of a short queue of people who were waiting to get through. All were pedestrians, for vehicles had been stopped and confiscated farther back. He had no difficulty in passing the Norwegian guards. His difficulty would be at the next barrier—the entrance to Sweden—a few paces ahead.

In the queue everyone was talking at once, talking to anybody, as always happens when danger is a common enemy. There were even two or three English people there. Actually Biggles found himself next to an American tourist—who had chosen a bad moment to visit Norway. He was bewailing the folly that had brought him from his own country, and cursed with hearty sincerity everybody responsible for the upheaval.

Slowly the queue shuffled forward towards the Swedish police and soldiers, who had come to reinforce the frontier guards. Some people were allowed through, but others were turned back. The man in front of Biggles was an elderly Norwegian, and Biggles waited with tense interest to see what would happen to him. He soon learned.

'Nationality?' snapped the passport officer.

'Norwegian.'

'Sorry, but you can't come through here.'

'But I must.' The man's voice was desperate.

'Why must you?'

The man poured out a score of reasons.

'Sorry, but we can't take in any more Norwegian refugees. Only foreigners passing through the country on their way home can be admitted, and they won't be allowed to stay in Sweden without a good reason.'

The man pleaded, but in vain. Sobbing, he was turned away.

Biggles had already realized that if he gave his nationality as Norwegian, he, too, would be stopped, so he switched his plan abruptly.

'Nationality?' questioned the officer.

'British.'

'Where are your papers?'

'Sorry, but I haven't any.'

The officer frowned. 'Why haven't you a passport?'

'I was in my hotel in Oslo when the Germans rushed in and seized everything,' answered Biggles readily, and this was no less than the truth. 'In the circumstances you can hardly blame me for not stopping to argue over my luggage. I reckoned I was lucky to get away at all.'

The officer bit his lip thoughtfully. 'So you've absolutely nothing to prove your identity?'

'Nothing, but I'm sure the British Consul will vouch for me if only you will let me see him.'

'Hmm.'

The officer was obviously in a quandary. It was clear that he didn't want to refuse admission to an Englishman; indeed, he had no reason to refuse; but, on the other hand, he didn't want to admit an enemy. If he admitted a man without papers he would be taking a serious risk.

Biggles saw the man hesitating and pressed his case. 'I've plenty of money on me,' he announced. 'You can take charge of it so you won't be put to any expense on my account. All I ask is that you take me, under guard if you like, to the nearest British Consul, and allow him to vouch for me. After all, if he accepts responsibility for me you won't have anything to worry about.'

This was so obviously true that it carried the point. The officer drew a deep breath. 'All right,' he agreed, and beckoned to two policeman. 'Escort this traveller to Rodas,' he ordered. 'If the British Consul there will take responsibility for him you can get a receipt and leave him. Otherwise, bring him back here.'

Biggles almost gasped his relief as he passed through the narrow gate. He was more or less under arrest, but that did not worry him. He was free, free from the Nazis, and therefore free from worry. His one thought now was to get back to France. If there was one anxiety that lingered in his mind, then it was fear that Sweden, too, might be invaded before he could get out of the country.

He was put in a car and taken to Rodas, less than half an hour's journey, and thence to the British Vice-Consulate. The Vice-Consul was still in his office, so Biggles introduced himself without loss of time, asking to be taken under protection.

Biggles stood in front of the two Swedes, so they did not see him drop an eyelid meaningly. The Vice-Consul did, however, and, realizing that there was more in the case than appeared on the surface, asked the guards to wait outside. He said he would take responsibility.

As soon as they were out of the door Biggles confessed everything. 'Believe me, I'm glad to be out of that,' he concluded feelingly.

The Vice-Consul was interested, as he had every reason to be, for queer things were happening in Scandinavia. Over a cigarette and a cup of coffee Biggles told the whole story, quietly and concisely, holding nothing back, as a sick man might explain his symptoms to a doctor.

'My word! You were certainly lucky to get out,' said the Vice-Consul when he had finished. 'I expect you want to get straight back home?'

'You bet I do!' returned Biggles. 'The sooner I let Colonel Raymond know where I am the better.'

The Vice-Consul looked up sharply. 'Would you like to speak to him?'

'Speak to him? How?' Biggles was amazed.

'On the telephone.'

'Can you get through to London?'

'Of course. Sweden isn't at war—at least, not yet.'

Biggles was delighted. 'Why, that's fine'

'I'll get Raymond for you,' the Vice-Consul promised.

He was as good as his word, but there was a long delay before Biggles found himself speaking to the Colonel. In a few words he told him what had happened, describing how he had narrowly escaped serving as a traitor Norwegian in the Nazi Air Force. Even before he had finished a doubt crept into his mind, a doubt as to whether he was wise in telling the Colonel this now. It would have been better to wait until he got home. The Colonel might ask him. . . .

The Colonel *did* ask him. Biggles knew instantly what was coming from the sudden change in Colonel Raymond's voice.

'You know what I'm going to ask you to do?' said the Colonel.

Biggles hesitated. 'I've got a pretty good idea,' he said slowly. 'You want me to go back into Norway.'

'Yes. Fate or fortune has put an astounding opportunity your way. It's a chance that we ought not to lose. With you behind the German lines in Norway, serving as an officer in the Air Force, we should learn every move—'

'Oh, no,' interrupted Biggles curtly. 'I'm a pilot. I've had quite enough of Secret Service work.'

The Colonel made a longish speech in which he dwelt on the extraordinary opportunity that pure chance had put in Biggles' way, and the wonderful service he could render his country by going back.

'Of course,' he concluded sadly, 'I can't *order* you to

go. But, frankly, you're not the man I take you to be if you let this golden opportunity slip.'

'But I'm not a professional spy,' protested Biggles vigorously.

'My dear Bigglesworth, you yourself have seen what Germany is doing in Norway. There's black treachery for you, if you like. We've got to fight the enemy with his own weapons, if only for the sake of the Norwegians.'

Thus spoke the Colonel. It was a subtle argument that he put forward, put in such a way that Biggles could hardly refuse.

'All right,' he said at last, wearily. 'How am I going to get into touch with you when I have something to report?'

'Leave that to me,' said the Colonel quickly. 'I can't tell you now. Arrangements will have to be made, but you'll get further instructions in due course. Get back to the aerodrome and learn all you can about the enemy's movements.'

'Just one request,' put in Biggles. 'I feel very much on my own up here; if you could get Lacey and Hebblethwaite somewhere handy, somewhere where I could reach them in emergency, I'd be grateful. As you know, we always work as a team, and I need a little moral support, anyway. If they hear nothing they'll be worried to death about me.'

'I'll get them within striking distance of you at once,' promised the Colonel without hesitation. 'As a matter of fact, knowing things were warming up, I brought them home from France yesterday, since when they've been waiting on the East Coast ready to slip across in case you needed help. They can be over in a couple of hours.'

'But how can I make contact with them?'

'I shall have to think about that, but I'll arrange something immediately, don't worry. Good luck. I mustn't hold the line any longer.' The Colonel rang off.

The Vice-Consul heard Biggles' end of the conversation, of course. He shrugged his shoulders sympathetically.

'Bad luck, old man,' he said quietly. 'But you must admit that Colonel Raymond is right. It is on such chances as this that wars are sometimes won or lost. How do you propose getting back into Norway?'

'I think the easiest way would be for you to refuse to accept responsibility for me,' suggested Biggles readily. 'In that case the Swedes will soon have me back across the frontier.'

The Vice-Consul nodded and pressed the bell. The two policemen came back into the room.

'I have had a conversation with this—er—applicant,' said the Vice-Consul coolly. 'He may be telling the truth, but he has no means of proving it, so in your interests as well as mine I'd rather not accept responsibility.'

'You'll leave him with us to deal with then?' said the senior of the two police.

'Yes, I'm afraid no other course is open to me.'

The officer tapped Biggles on the arm. 'Come,' he said.

Obediently, Biggles followed.

Half an hour later he was gently but firmly shown across the frontier back into Norway. He made no demur. It would have been a waste of time even if he had wanted to stay in Sweden. For a while he walked slowly down the road, but as soon as he was out of sight of the frontier post he quickened his steps and made his way to where he had left the motor-cycle. It was still there, so he dragged it out and recovered his swastika armlet from under the saddle. Deep in thought, he started the engine. Reaching the main road, he turned away from the frontier and headed back towards Boda, back towards the enemy.

He had no difficulty in getting back—his swastika flags saw to that. As he dismounted near the clubhouse Kristen hurried towards him.

'Hello,' he said curiously. 'Where have you been?'

'Only for a ride,' answered Biggles casually. 'Why?'

'Baron von Leffers has been asking for you.'

Biggles nodded. 'I'll report to him at once,' he said quietly.

# Chapter 4
# Cross-Examined

Biggles found von Leffers in his office. He was not
alone. Two other men were there. One was the man
whose motor-cycle he had got; the other was an elderly,
hard-faced civilian whose pugnacious jaw, gimlet eyes,
and arrogant bearing bespoke an official of importance.
His grey hair had been cropped so short that he
appeared to be completely bald. Biggles guessed to
what department he belonged before he was introduced.

Baron von Leffers stared at Biggles stonily. 'Leutnant
Hendrik, this is Oberleutnant* Ernst von Hymann,' he
said curtly, waving a hand towards the stranger. 'He
is a senior officer of the Gestapo. He wishes to speak
to you. You have kept him waiting.'

'I'm very sorry, sir, but I didn't know he was here,'
returned Biggles contritely.

To his infinite relief the Commandant did not ask
where he had been. He left it to the Gestapo officer to
continue the conversation.

Von Hymann invited Biggles to be seated, and then
stood up, legs apart, to face him squarely. In some
strange way he reminded Biggles of a mangy bulldog.
When he spoke his voice was brittle.

'Leutnant Hendrik,' he began, 'earlier to-day when

* German rank equivalent to Lieutenant in the army or Flying officer
in the Air force.

39

you were interviewed by the Commandant of this aerodrome you gave him certain particulars of your flying career. Among other things you said that you had been a pilot in America, and more lately in Canada. Is that correct?'

'Quite correct, sir.'

'As you may have heard,' continued von Hymann, 'we make a point of checking up on every statement made by aliens. You, as a Norwegian, come into that category.'

'But—'

'We shall get on faster if you leave me' to ask the questions.'

Biggles bowed.

'You further stated that when you were in Canada you were employed as an air pilot.'

'Correct.'

'And you were once employed by a firm called Arctic Airways located at Fort Beaver?'

'Quite right.*'

Von Hymann crouched like a wild beast about to spring.

'We have been unable to confirm that you ever had any connexion with Arctic Airways.'

Biggles remained calm. 'To whom did you go for your information?'

'Our agents in Canada have been through the official records. We also have newspaper reports of the scandal in which the company was involved.'

'You mean the stealing of the Moose Creek gold?'

Von Hymann relaxed slightly. 'Well, you do at least

---

* In making this statement Biggles was stating the truth. See *Biggles Flies North*.

know something about it,' he conceded. 'Yes, that was what I meant.'

Biggles had, of course, flown for Arctic Airways, so he knew all about the incident, as well as the company's affairs. But it had been under his own name, so he could understand why the German agents in Canada had failed to find any particulars of a pilot named Hendrik. However, since he, Biggles, knew all about the company, and all that he had said concerning it was true, he was not unduly alarmed by the cross-examination to which he was being subjected. But then he did not know what it was leading up to.

Von Hymann continued. 'In the reports concerning Arctic Airways we can find no record of a pilot by the name of Hendrik.'

'That's quite likely,' remarked Biggles coolly. 'It is unlikely that any record would be kept. Pilots were always coming and going. I imagine that the only ones whose names were noted in the files were those mentioned in the newspapers in connexion with the gold robbery'

'Can you name the pilots chiefly concerned?'

The atmosphere in the room was now tense, and Biggles perceived what was coming. He had just been asked a leading question, for if it were true that he had flown for Arctic Airways he would—or should—be able to name the pilots.

'Certainly,' he replied easily. 'Arctic Airways was run by a fellow named Wilkinson, an Englishman who established a base aerodrome at Fort Beaver. The trouble started when a fellow named McBain tried to grab the aerodrome, bringing with him two pilots and

41

two German transport planes. His pilots were both ex-crooks. One was named Sarton and the other Feroni.'

Von Hymann nodded. 'What about Wilkinson's pilots?'

Biggles thought for a moment. 'There was a chap named Graves—he was killed, I remember. Then there was Lacey, and—oh yes, a lad named Hebblethwaite—or some such name.'

'Anybody else?'

Biggles saw the trap clearly now, but his expression did not change.

'Yes, there was another fellow—a fellow with a curious name—Tigglesworth—or was it Nigglesworth?'

'Was it Bigglesworth?'

Biggles started. 'That's right—funny name.'

'You must have seen something of him?'

Biggles's pulses were beginning to beat faster. He didn't like the trend of the conversation, but he still hoped there was nothing serious behind it. One slip, though, and he was lost. An expression of anxiety on his face would be noted at once by the cold eyes that were fixed on his in unwavering intensity.

'Oh, yes, I often saw Bigglesworth,' he admitted.

'Would you know him again if you saw him?'

'I should think so. Of course, this Arctic Airways business happened some time ago, but if he hasn't grown a beard or anything like that, I think I should know him at once.'

'Could you describe him?'

'More or less. He was a slim fellow with fair hair—rather sharp features. As a matter of fact, he was about my build.'

Von Hymann glanced at a paper that he held in his hand. 'He must have been very much like you.'

Biggles smiled. 'Nobody has ever mistaken me for him,' he observed lightly. 'Why all this about Bigglesworth—do you know him?'

Von Hymann ignored the question. Instead, he asked another.

'Do you know what became of him subsequently?'

Biggles shrugged. 'How should I? I believe he went back to England, but I wouldn't swear to it.'

The German's manner became grim. 'I'll tell you what he did. He returned to England and set up as a free-lance pilot, and while he did a certain amount of casual work, in reality he was the British Intelligence Service's chief flying agent.'

Biggles made a grimace. 'I shouldn't have thought that was much in his line—he always struck me as being a nervous sort of fellow.'

'It seems that it was very much in his line. Not long ago he was in Finland. We now have reason to believe that he has transferred his unwelcome attentions to Norway.'

'You mean—he is actually in Norway?'

'This morning he was seen in Oslo by one of our agents.'

'Why didn't you pick him up?'

'Unfortunately the agent lost him in the crowd—the fool.'

Biggles nodded. 'Pity. But what has all this got to do with me?' he asked.

'I will tell you. The man who saw Bigglesworth has dashed back to Berlin to get further particulars about him from Hauptmann von Stalhein,* who has had more to do with him than anyone else. In the meantime, he is the only man on my staff who could recognize Bigglesworth if he saw him, so I want you to go into Oslo and see if you can find him. We've rounded up a lot of suspects; if he isn't among them you had better search the hotels and the streets until you find him.'

'I don't care much for this sort of thing. I really wanted to do some flying,' protested Biggles as cautiously as he dared.

'There will be time for that later. At the moment you are under my orders. Go to Oslo at once. You can stay at an hotel. If you see Bigglesworth, don't let him out of your sight. Call the first soldiers you see and have him arrested. You had better take that armlet of and put it in your pocket for the time being, so as not to attract attention to yourself.'

'Very well, sir. But if I don't wear an armlet will the soldiers accept my orders? Isn't there a risk of my being taken into custody myself?'

'I was prepared for that.' Von Hymann took a small, square card from his pocket. It was printed in red and black, and bore the number 2001. 'That is a pass, signed by myself,' continued the German. 'It will take you anywhere without question. While you are working for me you will not use your name; use your official number.'

Biggles noted the number and put the Gestapo pass in his pocket. 'Suppose I want to get into touch with you, sir?'

* Captain von Stalhein. For Biggles' first contact with von Stalhein see *Biggles Flies East* now published by Red Fox.

'My head-quarters are at the Hôtel Port, on the waterfront.'

'If I don't find Bigglesworth at once, how long do you want me to go on looking for him?'

'Until you hear from me again.'

'Very good, sir. I'll attend to it, but—if I may be allowed to say so—I hope you won't keep me on the job too long. As a pilot, naturally, I'm anxious to get into the air, in which respect I should be useful, for I know the country pretty well. Moreover, as you know, I have had experience of flying over similar country and in similar weather conditions in northern Canada.'

'I'll bear it in mind,' returned von Hymann crisply. He turned to the Commandant. 'Have you any questions for Hendrik?'

'No.'

'That's all then.'

Biggles risked a last question, for the information would be valuable to him if he could get it. 'What is the name of your man who knows Bigglesworth?' he inquired. 'I ask because it might be a good thing if we met some time, and compared notes.'

'Brandt.'

'Thank you, sir.' Biggles saluted and departed.

As he closed the door behind him he drew a deep breath and moistened his lips with his tongue, for they had gone dry during the strain of the interview. For a moment he stood still, getting his nerves under control. They had not failed him during the difficult cross-examination, but the inevitable reaction, now that the immediate danger had passed, left him slightly weak. At the same time he endeavoured to adjust his ideas to meet the new situation.

'Suffering rattlesnakes! Where am I getting to?' he murmured, a ghost of a smile softening his face. 'First I'm sworn in the German Air Force; now, of all things, I'm a full-blown Gestapo agent. I've done some strange jobs in my life, but this is the first time I've had to look for myself.' Then his face hardened again, for he realized that that might well be a more difficult, and more dangerous, task than it sounded.

He went to the dining-room and had a quiet bite of supper. Then he found Kristen, with whom he was anxious to keep in touch, for he made a point of neglecting nothing and nobody who might be of service to him. Without divulging his mission he told Kristen that he had got to go into Oslo on temporary duty, and would probably stay at the Hotel Kapital. Kristen was curious, but knowing who von Hymann was, asked no questions concerning Biggles's task.

'How are you going to get to Oslo?' he inquired.

'I've got a motor-bike; I will use that,' returned Biggles.

An hour later he was in Oslo, parking the motorcycle in the hotel garage. The manager was still there, and recognized him. He said that the room Biggles had previously used was still available, and as this suited Biggles he decided to take it. At the foot of the stairs he was stopped by two men who stepped out of the shadows.

'Who are you?' asked one of them curtly.

Biggles showed his Gestapo pass, and the power of it was instantly apparent, for not only did the two men withdraw hastily, but they apologized for troubling him—a rare concession for Nazis.

Biggles continued on up the stairs, deep in thought.

He was most worried by the knowledge that in the same city as himself there had been a man who knew him by sight. True, from what von Hymann had said, the man was now in Germany. But how long would it be before, he returned? Obviously, not long. Moreover, he had gone to see von Stalhein, Biggles' arch-enemy, the man of all men whom he had the greatest cause to fear. The report that he, Biggles, was in Norway would probably be quite sufficient to bring von Stalhein to Oslo at top speed. In an aeroplane he could make the journey in two or three hours. He might even now be on his way to Norway. Indeed, for all Biggles knew, he might already be in Oslo; it all depended on how long Brandt had been gone, and the precise hour of his departure was something Biggles did not know. He knew the man's name, and that was something; but he didn't even know him by sight.

Worn out by the day's exertions and anxieties, Biggles flung himself on his bed just as he was to rest. He wanted to sleep, but his racing brain made it impossible. From far to the north came the low roar of bursting bombs; he could feel the thud and vibrations of the explosions; and as the window-panes rattled his face hardened with anger.

'Well, I'm here, and if I can put a spoke in the wheel of the savages who drop bombs on helpless civilians I certainly will,' he mused grimly.

The suspense of not knowing what was happening, or if Brandt had returned, became intolerable, and, unable to rest, he got up and looked at his watch. It was not yet eleven o'clock. Perhaps he would sleep better if. . . .

In a moment he had made up his mind. He would

find out if Brandt had returned. If he had, then he would be in a better position to know how to act. On the other hand, if Brandt was still in Germany, then he could at least reckon on a few hours' grace. How could he obtain the information? Obviously, there was only one way, one place, and that was at Gestapo head-quarters at the Hotel Port. By going there he might be putting his head into a noose, but anything was better than this gnawing anxiety, which would certainly impair his usefulness to Colonel Raymond.

He put on his hat and went out. The same two men were in the hall, but they only nodded to him. There were few people in the streets, and no taxis, so he had to walk to his objective — not that that mattered, for it was only a short distance away. German troops were everywhere, particularly near the waterfront, where stores and guns were being unloaded. Biggles surveyed them with eyes trained by long experience; he noted particularly the number of guns and their calibres, the types of vehicles, and the quantities of other stores. He was stopped twice by plain-clothes men and ques-tioned, from which he was able to gather an idea of the precautions being taken to prevent useful infor-mation from reaching the Norwegian troops, who—so he learned from snatches of conversation between passers-by—were putting up a spirited resistance farther north. However, in each case the production of his Gestapo pass acted like magic, and he went on to the Hotel Port.

Two storm-troopers were on duty outside the main entrance. They stopped him, of course, and asked his business.

Biggles smiled and showed his ever-ready pass. 'Perhaps you can help me, and save me worrying people while they are busy—as I see they are,' he said. 'Do either of you know Herr Brandt by sight?'

One of the men said he did.

'Is he back yet, do you know?'

'Yes,' answered the man unhesitatingly. 'He came in about half an hour ago. He came by plane—there it is.' He pointed to a civil flying-boat that rested on the placid water, slightly apart from a number of military marine aircraft.

'Was he alone?' queried Biggles.

'No, there was another man with him.'

'You don't know his name?'

'No.'

'Was he by any chance a thin man, with sharp features, wearing a monocle?'

'Yes, that's right,' agreed the man.

'I see,' said Biggles casually.

'You can go in if you want to speak to them,' invited the trooper.

Brandt and von Stalhein were the very last two people on earth Biggles wanted to see at that moment, but he did not say so.

'They're probably tired after their journey,' he remarked, yawning. 'I'm tired myself. I'll call again in the morning. Phew! What a day it's been.'

The storm-trooper grinned. 'You're right there.'

'What's happening, d'you know?'

'They say we've got most of the country except Narvik. There's a rumour that British troops are being landed there.'

This was welcome information, and Biggles made a note of it. He chatted for a few minutes, learning where

49

the Norwegians were resisting the German advance, and picking up scraps of news about the German forces, concerning which the two storm-troopers were quite ready to boast.

All the while he was talking he was standing in a position from which he could see through the glass-panelled doors into the vestibule beyond. And it was a good thing that he did so, for, suddenly, from the foot of the stairs, appeared two men. One he did not know, but the other was his old enemy, Erich von Stalhein of the German Secret Service. Both were dressed as if they were going out.

Biggles tarried no longer. 'Well, I'll get along and see about some sleep,' he announced. 'It looks as if we shall have a busy day again to-morrow. Good-night.'

He walked away, but turning into a lane between two warehouses, watched the door of the hotel. He had not long to wait. A few minutes later von Stalhein and the other man—who he presumed was Brandt—came out, and walked briskly along the waterfront. From his retreat Biggles watched them pass within ten yards of him. They were talking animatedly, but in tones too low for him to catch what they said. As soon as they had got some distance ahead he followed them.

At first he was glad that they took a direction which suited him, for it was the direction of his own hotel. It did not occur to him that they were actually going to the hotel until, from the opposite pavement, they walked straight across to the entrance and disappeared through the swing doors.

Now Biggles, having stayed in it, knew the hotel well. He knew all the entrances—there were three, including a luggage entrance. Walking past the front door he saw the two Germans in the hall talking to the hotel manager, so hastening his steps, he hurried to a side entrance which he knew also led to the hall. But he did not go right in, for he wanted to know what the Germans were saying. He opened the door quietly and took a few paces along a corridor until he could hear their voices.

The trend of the conversation was much what he expected. Brandt was describing 'Bigglesworth', and asking the hotel manager if he knew anything of him. The manager replied, of course, in the negative. He declared that the only person in the hotel who fitted the description was a Norwegian named Hendrik, who, at the moment, was out. On receipt of this information the two Germans announced that they would wait for him to come back, and made themselves comfortable on a settee.

As there was no further point in remaining, Biggles returned to the street. He found a café still open, and sat at a side table over a cup of coffee to ponder his position, which he felt was getting desperate. Brandt and von Stalhein were now looking for Hendrik, all because the quick-witted Brandt had unfortunately caught a glimpse of him. Still, this did not necessarily mean that either he or von Stalhein now believed Hendrik to be Bigglesworth, but the very fact that they were anxious to interview Hendrik proved that they were suspicious. Once they saw him the game would be up, so if he remained in Oslo it was certain that sooner or later they would find him.

For a little while he could not make up his mind what to do for the best. There were moments when he felt inclined to devote his entire energy to getting out of the country, for which Colonel Raymond could hardly blame him, for when he had agreed to remain the position had been altogether different. At that time he had been simply a renegade Norwegian, and in no immediate danger. He was not suspected of being Bigglesworth, and von Stalhein had not been in the country. Yet, on the other hand, he felt that with his Gestapo pass in his pocket, never before had he been in such an admirable position to gather information, information that might well be of vital importance to the Allies. In short, he felt it would be insane to remain, yet despicable to run away—even if he could. But he would certainly have to get out of Oslo. That, of course, would make von Hymann suspicious, and perhaps start a hue and cry. What excuse could he give for leaving the city?

Sitting there alone in a quiet corner he worked out a plan; a plan which, if successful, might answer a lot of questions for him. The weakness of it lay in his abandoning—at least for the time being—the aerodrome at Boda, for it was clear from what Colonel Raymond had said that he was going to get in touch with him there, presumably by means of a secret agent. In the end Biggles decided that this could not be avoided. He got up, paid his bill, and went along to the garage at the corner of the street. It was, of course, owned by a Norwegian, so the wretched man was in no case to resist German demands. Biggles said he was a member of the Gestapo and demanded a car.

The proprietor raised no objection. He pointed to an Opel saloon. 'Will that do?'

'Yes. Are the tanks full?'

'Yes.'

Without another word Biggles got in the car and drove slowly out of the city. He was stopped several times, but his pass always carried him through. Reaching the suburbs, he pulled up outside a telephone call box and rang up the Hotel Port, giving his number and asking for Oberleutnant von Hymann.

He was told that von Hymann had been in, but had gone out again.

Having ascertained that he was speaking to a Gestapo operator, Biggles then asked if he could leave a message, and was told that he might.

'Take it down,' he ordered. 'My number is 2001. Say that I have located Bigglesworth. He has left the city in a car, heading northward. At the garage where he got the car he asked how far it was to Narvik, so that is presumably where he is bound for. I'm following him, and am not far behind. I'll report again at the first opportunity. Got that?'

The operator read over the message.

'That's right,' confirmed Biggles, and hung up. He went back to the car. For a minute or two he studied the map which he always kept in his pocket; then he drove on, heading northward, whence came the sounds of battle.

53

# Chapter 5
## Unexpected Allies

In acting as he did, Biggles was actuated first and
foremost by the obvious necessity for getting out of
Oslo; also he wanted time to think, to muster the many
features and various aspects of his position. And this,
presently, he did, having turned into a by-road for the
purpose. He stopped the car so that he could concentrate on the problem.

Slowly the situation clarified itself into a number of
issues, all governed by the outstanding fact that not
only was it known to the Gestapo that Squadron Leader
Bigglesworth was in Norway, but von Stalhein was also
in Norway for the purpose of finding him. Von Stalhein
and Brandt knew him by sight, so it would be merely
foolish to hope that he could continue to move about
the country without being spotted. To carry on espion-
age work in such conditions would impose a strain not
lightly to be borne, a strain that would certainly impair
his activities as well as his efficiency. He felt that if
Colonel Raymond knew this, he could hardly fail to
ask him to leave the country. The trouble was that he
had no means of getting in touch with the Colonel
except by again crossing the frontier into Sweden. Yet,
apart from the obvious risks involved in such a pro-
cedure, such a course would be letting Colonel Raymond down, for the Colonel, acting under the assumption that he was in Norway, might be making all sorts

of plans, the success of which depended on his being at Boda. Raymond was even then taking steps to get into touch with him at the aerodrome, and would expect him to be there. If the secret agent arrived at the aerodrome and failed to find him, the consequences might be tragic. All of which meant that he ought to return to the aerodrome. But now, apart from Oslo, the aerodrome was the most dangerous place in the country. Von Stalhein and Brandt were interested in Hendrik, whose failure to return to the hotel would only deepen their suspicions. They would continue their search vigorously, and it could only be a question of time before they—or someone—discovered that a Norwegian named Hendrik had joined the Nazi Air Force at Boda. Von Stalhein's agile brain would instantly perceive what had happened, and that would be the end.

A further point not to be overlooked was this. He was supposed to be acting under von Hymann's orders, and while his telephone message might be sufficient to allay suspicion for the time being, unless he showed up pretty soon, or reported again, von Hymann, too, would start wondering what had happened to Hendrik.

Now in introducing the town of Narvik into his message to von Hymann Biggles was prompted by one reason only. From scraps of conversation overheard he had gathered that a British force was landing there. British troops might be landing at other places as well for all he knew, but owing to the suddenness of the German attack the whole country was in a state of confusion. Nobody seemed to know what was happening.

At the back of Biggles' mind, when he had rung up

to speak to von Hymann, was a vague idea of getting 'Bigglesworth' out of the country. That is to say, if he could lead von Hymann to believe that Bigglesworth had fled the country, via the British-held port of Narvik—a not unreasonable possibility—then the hue and cry would die down. Von Stalheim would be informed and would probably return to Germany. Brandt might go, too, leaving Biggles to do his work in a less unhealthy atmosphere. So, if this could be brought about, it would be a useful stroke of work. But could it? Obviously, it was not going to be easy to get to Narvik, or anywhere else for that matter, for not only were more and more German troops arriving in the country, but the Norwegians themselves were mobilizing and putting up a stiff resistance. So it seemed that he would have to pose as a Gestapo agent when talking to the Germans, and as a Norwegian when intercepted by Norwegians. He would have to adopt a dual personality. He still had a Norwegian passport as well as his Gestapo ticket, so he could use either as circumstances demanded, and as he was still in civilian clothes he felt that this ought to be possible.

There was one final point that worried him. In Oslo he had picked up information which the British authorities would be glad to have, but this information would be of no value unless he could pass it on immediately, for the position was changing every few hours. Could he reach the British forces? He did not know, but he could try. If he succeeded in getting into the town of Narvik he would get a message through to von Hymann from there, to the effect that Bigglesworth had escaped. At the same time he would ask permission to return to Boda, and stay there until he got Colonel

Raymond's permission to leave the country. He was anxious, desperately anxious, to get out, not so much on account of the danger of his task as his dislike for the work he was doing. Spying as a profession had no appeal to him, although more than once he had been forced to do it. In the present case only a sequence of unforeseen circumstances had combined to thrust him, against his will, into the unenviable position in which he now found himself. He much preferred the straightforward life of a fighting pilot, which, really, was what he was.

He looked again at his map, noted the shortest way to his objective, started the car, and set off on his long journey.

Biggles covered fifty miles in fair time, although, as was inevitable, he was stopped several times by German patrols, but on the production of his pass he was allowed to proceed. Once he found himself near some brisk fighting and took refuge in a peasant's cottage—posing, of course, as a Norwegian. The peasant told him of a detour by which he could avoid the battle, and he lost no time in taking it. Now, having passed the extremity of the German forces, he started to run into Norwegian patrols, who also stopped him. But when he showed his Norwegian passport, and said that he was on his way to Narvik to offer his services to the British, no obstacle was put in his path. The noise of war died away behind him, but progress was slow on account of the state of the road, particularly in the passes where the snow was still deep. Naturally, the farther north he got the more arctic the conditions became, and once he was compelled to wait for a snowstorm to blow itself out before he could go on. He was desperately tired, but matters were too urgent for him to rest—at least, for the time being.

On and on he drove into the darkness of the night. He passed a signpost pointing to Trondheim, away to the west. There was firing there, too, but who was responsible for it he did not know, for he was still unaware that Germans had landed at several places on the coast. Leaving Trondheim far behind, and reaching a village called Stol, he halted. He was so weary that he was beginning to sway in his seat. To proceed farther in his present state would be to court disaster by accident, so he went to the inn. The landlord and his wife were still up; several villagers were there too, all discussing the calamity that had befallen their country. Biggles introduced himself—as Hendrik, of course—said that he was on government service and was on his way to Narvik. He was worn out, so could he have a bed for the rest of the night?

The kindly souls assured him that he might, but would he please tell them what was happening in Oslo? They had a wireless set, but they knew it was in German hands and they were anxious to know the truth. Biggles told them as much as he thought was good for them. Afterwards he fell on his bed and slept the sleep of exhaustion.

As soon as it was daylight he had a good breakfast and continued his journey. The scenery had always been wild, but now it grew rugged in the extreme, far more savage than it had seemed from the air. On all sides towered mountains, gaunt, still white with snow. The lower slopes bristled with countless conifers. For the most part the road ran through valley or gorge, but not infrequently it followed a cornice round the mountain side so that sheer cliff rose on the one hand and a fathomless void dropped away on the other. The surface of the road got worse and worse.

But Biggles was not concerned with these details. He was concerned only with reaching his objective, which had become a sort of mania. Once, from an eminence, he caught a distant view of the sea far away to the left, and he knew that he was now in the narrow northern end of Norway. Shortly afterwards the road struck a fiord, one of the many deep-thrusting arms of the sea for which Norway is famous, and thereafter it more or less followed the coast. He breathed a sigh of relief when, from the top of a hill, he saw a town in the distance that he knew could only be the port for which he was bound.

He might not have seen the sailors had not one of them deliberately exposed himself, making strange signals. Biggles stopped at once. As the man drew near—he was little more than a lad—Biggles saw that he wore the uniform of an officer of the British Mercantile Marine. It was dirty and torn.

The man came nearer. 'Me British sailor,' he said, pointing to the braid on his sleeve. Then he pointed to his mouth. 'Me hungry—no food,' he continued.

That he was telling the truth was obvious for his face was pinched and pale. It was apparent that he assumed Biggles to be a Norwegian, and therefore a friend.

Said Biggles, coolly, 'What on earth are you doing here?'

The sailor started violently. 'Great Scott! Are you a Britisher?' he asked joyfully.

Biggles did not answer the question. 'What are you doing here?' he repeated.

59

'We were torpedoed off the coast—the trawler *Sea-goer*.'

'We?'

'Yes. Me and some of the ship's company managed to swim ashore. That was two days ago. We've been on the run ever since—without a bite of food.'

'How many of you are there?'

'In my party—seven.'

'Why didn't you go to Narvik?'

The sailor stared. 'To Narvik? That's the last place we're likely to go—unless we're caught and taken there.'

Biggles sensed a disturbing implication in the statement. 'Why, what's wrong with Narvik?' he asked quickly.

'The Germans have got it.'

Biggles was speechless while this staggering piece of information sank in. 'But—but I thought the British had landed there?'

The sailor laughed harshly. 'There was talk of them landing there, but they're not there yet, you can take that from me. The fiord is stiff with Jerry destroyers. They've got the town.'

Biggles' scheme crashed to the ground. 'What are you trying to do?' he asked.

'Find someone to hide us until our fellows arrive, or else find a ship to pick us up. That's why we're sticking near the coast.'

'Do the Germans know you're ashore?'

'Unfortunately, yes. They've been chasing us.'

'Where are the rest of you?'

The sailor jerked his thumb over his shoulder. 'Hiding in a little dell.'

60

Instinctively Biggles glanced in the direction indicated, and as he did so a movement caught his eye. He looked again and saw that he had not been mistaken. A German soldier was creeping towards them, taking cover between the rocks. Others were there too, to left and right. Quickly Biggles looked behind him and saw more Germans advancing stealthily through the trees that cloaked the side of the hill.

'What's wrong?' asked the sailor sharply, taking alarm from the expression on Biggles's face.

'I'm afraid you're out of luck, old man,' returned Biggles quietly. 'We're surrounded. Are you armed?'

'We haven't a weapon between us.'

'Then you'd be wise to give yourselves up. There's no sense in throwing your lives away uselessly.'

'You're talking about us. What are you going to do?' asked the sailor suspiciously.

Biggles could already see a plan by which the incident might be turned to good account, but it depended largely on the courage and fortitude of the sailor. He drew his automatic.

'What the–' began the sailor aghast, but Biggles cut him short.

'Answer my questions quickly,' he said. 'I'm a British spy, and I'm going to put my life in your hands. I've got to get back to England with vital information. Got that?'

'Yes,' gasped the sailor.

'What's your name?'

'Evans — Bill Evans.'

'It's in your power to help me — and the country. Will you do it? You'll be taken prisoner, anyway, so it won't make things any worse for you.'

'What d'you want me to do?'

'First, put your hands up. That will lead the Jerries to think I've captured you.'

The sailor raised his hands.

Biggles went on quickly, for he could see the Germans fast closing in.

'They think I'm a German agent,' he said. 'After you're taken I shall come to question you. I shall ask if you had anyone else with your party. At first you will refuse to answer, but under pressure you'll admit that a Britisher named Bigglesworth attached himself to you. When I ask what's become of him you'll say he left you—stole a dinghy and rowed out to a steamer. Got the name right?'

'Bigglesworth.'

'That's it. Actually, I'm Bigglesworth, and I've got to make it look as if I've escaped out of the country— understand?'

'Yes.'

'Fine. That's all. Act as you never acted before. Remember, however tough your plight may seem, mine is a lot worse. One slip and it's a firing party for me.'

'By gosh! You've sure got a nerve,' muttered the sailor admiringly. 'I won't let you down.'

'Thanks, pal. If you get back home and I don't, find Colonel Raymond of British Intelligence and tell him that you saw me, and that I did my best. Prime your friends about Bigglesworth, but don't tell them more than you need, and on no account let them know it's me. Simply tell them to remember that Bigglesworth got away on a ship—a slim fellow with fair hair. Now take me to the others.'

Still with his hands up, Biggles walking close behind

him with the pistol raised, the sailor marched stiffly into the dell. The others sprang up in dismay when they appeared.

'Hands up, everybody,' ordered Biggles curtly. 'March out into the open in single file.'

'Do what you're told, boys,' said Evans tersely.

Slowly the weary sailors raised their hands, and at the expression on their faces Biggles nearly weakened. He would have much preferred to fight side by side with them.

'Out you go,' he said shortly.

At that moment the German troops sprang up and ran forward. An officer was at their head.

Biggles received them with a cold smile. 'You've arrived at a useful moment,' he said harshly, showing his Gestapo pass. 'I saw these fellows skulking among the rocks so I went after them. You'd better get them to a safe place.' As he spoke he took out his armlet and replaced it on his sleeve.

The German officer, who was quite young, was all politeness. 'Leave them to me,' he answered. 'Forgive me for saying so, but you shouldn't have risked your life as you did. These fellows are a desperate lot and they might have attacked you. We've been following them for some time, to round them up.'

'No harm done,' returned Biggles briefly. 'I must get on, so I'll leave you to finish the job.' With a curt nod he got back into his car and drove on into the town.

Even before he reached it he saw that what the sailor had told him was only too true. German troops were everywhere, and five destroyers lay in the fiord. There was also a number of flying-boats and seaplanes.

He went straight to General Head-quarters and

asked to see the officer in charge of operations. He had to wait a few minutes; then two senior naval officers came out and he was shown in.

A Colonel, with his adjutant at his elbow, received him coldly but politely. From their manner Biggles judged that they had little love for the Gestapo, but feared them too much to be anything but civil. He showed his pass.

'I'm looking for an English spy named Bigglesworth,' he said without wasting words. 'He bolted from Oslo, heading north. We have good reason to think that he was coming here. Have you any English prisoners?'

'Yes, we have a few.' The Colonel looked at his adjutant.

'Eighteen, sir, I think.'

'Have they been examined?' inquired Biggles.

'Of course.'

'Is Bigglesworth among them?'

'He may be, but if he is he didn't give that name,' answered the adjutant.

'I'd better see them,' said Biggles curtly.

The adjutant took him to a small schoolroom which was being used as a prison camp. Several sentries were on guard. The prisoners were paraded. They stood in a line, coldly hostile, defiant, in spite of the state they were in, for they all looked as if they had been through a bad time. There were one or two Air Force uniforms, but most of the men were sailors. One, a leathery-faced old salt, cursed Hitler and everything German in a steady stream of invective.

Biggles glanced at him. 'Shut up!' he snapped, 'or I'll give you something to curse about, *Schweinehund*.' He walked slowly along the line.

Now all this, of course, was merely play-acting, part of the scheme that had now crystallized in his mind. He would certainly not see the man he professed to be looking for, nor did he expect to recognize anyone; so he merely glanced at the faces as, with the adjutant and an armed soldier following, he walked slowly down the line. But when he came to the seventh man he stopped dead.

It was Algy.

# Chapter 6
# The Navy Arrives

How Biggles kept control of himself at that ghastly moment he never knew. For two palpitating seconds he stood stock still, while he felt the blood draining from his face. Then he walked on, looking for Ginger, who he felt must be there too. But of Ginger there was no sign, so he walked back along the line to Algy, feeling that he ought to make some excuse for stopping in front of him.

'Haven't I seen you before somewhere?' he asked harshly.

Algy didn't move a muscle. Actually, he had got over his shock at seeing Biggles, for he saw him immediately he entered the room—long before Biggles saw him.

'You may have seen my picture in the papers,' sneered Algy. 'I won the world championship at snakes and ladders—up one minute and down the next.'

There was a titter along the line.

Biggles spluttered with rage, German fashion. 'Silence!' he bellowed. Then he turned on his heel and walked away. 'He isn't here,' he told the adjutant. 'Let us go back to the Colonel—I must speak to him again.'

They returned to head-quarters.

'Did you find your man?' inquired the Colonel.

'No,' answered Biggles shortly. 'There'll be trouble if he gets away. He's a dangerous man. I must ring up my chief in Oslo.' He broke off and glanced over his

66

shoulder as from outside the door came the sound of quick footsteps. 'What's happening?' he asked.

The door opened. An N.C.O. came into the room and saluted. 'Seven more prisoners, sir,' he announced.

'Good,' said Biggles sharply. 'My man may be among them. Bring them in here—you don't mind, Colonel? I only want to see their faces.'

'Bring them in.'

The seven prisoners, the seven sailors whom Biggles had encountered on the hill-side, were marched in. Every face was expressionless.

Biggles scrutinized each man in turn. 'Who is the senior officer?' he snapped.

'I am,' growled Evans.

'Were there any more of you?'

Evans did not answer.

'Answer me!'

Still the sailor maintained a stubborn silence.

Biggles's jaw set in true Prussian fashion. 'I think you forget where you are,' he grated. 'I hope it will not be necessary for me to remind you. Were there more than seven in your party?'

Evans hesitated. 'There was one more, but he left us.'

'Why?'

'To get back to England, I suppose. He found a dinghy, and without waiting for us, rowed out to a steamer. But he wasn't really one of our party.'

'What do you mean?'

'As we walked down the coast we met him coming up. He said he had escaped from Oslo.'

Biggles affected a start. 'Oslo! What was his name?'

'He told me his name was Bigglesworth. He seemed

67

in a mighty hurry to get home. That's all I know about him.'

Biggles turned a grim face to the Colonel, who was watching the scene with intense interest.

'You heard that?' he said in a low voice. 'That was my man without a doubt. He must have left the road and gone down to the rocks; that was how I came to miss him. It looks as if he's got clean away. I'm afraid there will be trouble about this. I trust, sir, that you will confirm that I did everything possible in the time at my disposal? The man had gone before I got here. I'd better ring up my head-quarters at once. As you are the senior officer here perhaps you would be good enough to speak to my chief?' Biggles glanced at the escort. 'All right; I shan't want these prisoners again.'

As they filed away Biggles' eyes met those of Evans and flashed his thanks.

The Colonel had already picked up the telephone. He handed it to Biggles who put a call through to Gestapo head-quarters, at the Hotel Port, Oslo. When the operator spoke he asked for Oberleutnant von Hymann, and in a moment he was speaking to him.

'This is 2001, speaking from General Head-quarters, Narvik,' he said. 'I have to report that I tracked Bigglesworth to here, but he had left in a steamer before my arrival. I obtained this information from a party of British prisoners with whom Bigglesworth had for a short time been keeping company. One moment, sir, the Commanding Officer will speak to you. I am telephoning from his office.' Biggles handed the instrument to the Colonel.

There followed a long conversation in which the Colonel confirmed in detail all that Biggles had said, and added details of how the information had been obtained, remarking that he had been a witness of it. He asserted that everything possible had been done to apprehend the wanted man, but as he had left the country before steps could be taken to arrest him no fault could be attached to anyone. The conversation was concluded and the Colonel hung up the instrument. He turned to Biggles. 'Oberleutnant von Hymann says that you are to return to Boda at once,' he said.

'Very good, sir,' Biggles saluted and withdrew.

His plan had succeeded to the fullest possible extent, and but for one fly in the ointment he would have been elated. It was Algy.

What Algy was doing in Narvik, and how he had come to be taken prisoner, Biggles, of course, had no means of knowing; nor dare he risk arousing suspicion by making inquiries; but from the fact that he was in R.A.F. uniform Biggles could only conclude that, in accordance with his request to Colonel Raymond, Algy had been sent to Norway in an aeroplane with a view to getting into touch with him. If that were so, what had happened to Ginger? It seemed certain that they would start together. One fact was significant, and Biggles did not overlook it. Algy had come to Narvik, and that at once suggested that Narvik was to be the scene of British operations, otherwise he would not be so foolish as to land in territory held by the enemy. Again, if he, Algy, had come to Narvik, then there was good reason to suppose that something was in the wind, that some plan had been evolved to bring Biggles to the same place, in order that they could make contact. But it was a problem no amount of reasoning could answer; the facts could only be obtained from Algy himself. The point paramount in Biggles' mind was that von Hymann had ordered him to return to Boda, and to Boda he would have to go or lay himself open to dangerous questioning when he next saw the Gestapo chief. Yet he could not contemplate departing from Narvik leaving Algy a prisoner in German hands.

He was still standing near the wharf pondering this difficult problem when a German flying-boat appeared round a bend in the fiord, flying very low and at terrific speed. It was obvious that the pilot's mission was an urgent one. With professional interest Biggles watched the machine land and taxi quickly to the wharf where the other machines were moored. Even before the aircraft had stopped moving the pilot had scrambled out, shouting something in a voice that was hoarse with excitement. Instantly all was confusion.

Biggles hurried forward. 'What is it?' he asked a soldier, for he had not caught the pilot's words.

'British destroyers are coming up the fiord—five of them,' shouted the soldier as he dashed towards headquarters.

Biggles' pulses began to race. Things were going to happen in Narvik, that was certain. What part was he to play?

His first thought was not for himself nor for Algy; it was for the destroyers. Was the Commander of the flotilla aware that six German destroyers lay in the fiord? If so, did he know where they were? They were not all in the open water. Some were hidden behind promontories of rock, where their presence would not be suspected. The British destroyers might be steaming into a trap, and if so his first duty ought to be to warn them, regardless of anything else.

These were the thoughts that flashed through Biggles' mind in that tense moment, and it did not take him long to reach a decision. The Dornier flying-boat from which the German had landed was still floating on the water where its pilot had left it. Nobody was bothering about it, which was hardly surprising, for everyone was much too engrossed in other affairs. Sailors were rushing back to their ships. Pilots were running to their moorings; some were already taxi-ing higher up the fiord to get out of the way of the storm which they guessed was coming. Anti-aircraft gunners were hurrying to their posts. Troops were taking up positions, mounting machine-guns at points overlooking the fiord.

Biggles walked calmly down to the Dornier. A German pilot getting into a near-by machine had time to notice him, possibly because he was in civilian clothes.

'What are you going to do?' he shouted.

'Have a look at these *Englander*,' answered Biggles promptly.

'Can you fly?'

Biggles laughed. 'Watch me! I've just brought a message up from Oslo.'

The German had no further time to waste on idle curiosity so he turned away. Biggles got into the Dornier and started the engine. Then, sitting quietly in his seat, he tore a page out of his notebook and wrote a message. On another sheet he made a rough sketch-map of the inner fiord, showing where the German destroyers were waiting. This done, he put both pages in his silver cigarette case and slipped it back in his pocket. A quick glance round revealed that the position ashore remained unaltered, so he eased open the throttle and surged towards the open water. Another moment and his keel was cutting a line of white foam across it. As soon as he was in the air he turned, and, flying low, raced down the fiord.

He saw the British destroyers at once, for they were only about three miles away, steaming at high speed. They saw him, too—or the anti-aircraft gunners did, for instantly the air around him was filled with smoke, lacerated with flame and hurtling metal. With white face and set lips he swerved, dived and zoomed, anything to spoil the gunners' aim; but he still held on towards the ships.

His plan was to drop the cigarette case, with its message, on the deck of the leading destroyer, but such was the inferno that had broken out around him that he felt it was attempting the impossible. Apart from the ack ack fire, he knew it was no use trying to achieve his object by dropping the case while travelling in the opposite direction to the destroyers, for he would pass over them in a split second; his only chance was to overshoot them, turn, and then, travelling as slowly as possible, drop the message while going in the same direction.

For the next two minutes he became a machine, a part of the aircraft. His brain concentrated on one thought only, but it was not easy. Shells burst in front of him, beside him, above and below him, causing the Dornier to rock like a leaf in a gale. It quivered and shuddered as pieces of flying metal ripped through wings and fuselage. Pieces of fabric streamed aft, and he fully expected the machine to break up at any moment. He had never known an aircraft to stand up to such punishment.

He had a brief respite after he had flashed past the ships, for he was flying nearly on the water, and the gunners had not had time to turn their weapons.

Steeling himself for the ordeal that lay before him, he banked vertically and started back, using the smoke thrown out by the destroyers as a screen as far as this was possible. The acrid fumes stung his eyes and made him cough as they bit into his lungs, but he gritted his teeth and held on, telling himself that it could only last another minute; then, one way or the other, it would be over.

In a sort of hazy dream he counted the destroyers as he flashed over them, for his obective was the leader. One—two—three—four—the stern of the fifth came into view. With savage determination he jammed the joystick forward and dived into the very muzzles of the guns. His arm, with the cigarette case clutched in his hand, projected over the side. His fingers jerked open. The silver case flashed down. He saw it hit the deck, bounce, and slide to a standstill. Then he was past. But not unscathed. His port wing was wobbling and his engine was back-firing furiously. Black, oily smoke spurted out of it. Hot oil drove against the wind-screen, blinding him. The stench of petrol vapour struck his nostrils, and he pushed the joystick forward, tilting his nose towards the water. The engine coughed, and stopped. Leaning over the side, he saw that he was almost on the water; he jerked the joystick back, but he was a fraction of a second too late. The hull struck the placid surface of the fiord with a crash, and the machine bounced high. For a moment it hung in the air, wallowing like a wounded seagull, then it stalled. There was another crash as it struck the water. The Dornier at once began to sink as water poured through a score of holes.

Half dazed, Biggles scrambled out of the cockpit on to the back of the splinter-riddled hull. But in his heart he felt that his case was hopeless, for the leading destroyer was within a hundred yards, bearing straight down on him at a speed that would drive the knife-like bows through the flimsy aircraft like an axe. There was nothing he could do except hang on with one hand and wave with the other, although it seemed futile.

As it happened, it was not. The destroyer altered her course a fraction, revealing a party of sailors crowding near the rail. The vessel was, of course, too close to stop, even if the Commander had wished to do so— which in the circumstances was hardly likely. But a rope coiled out. Well and truly thrown, it fell across the fuselage, now half submerged by the bow-wave. Half smothered with spray, Biggles grabbed the line and gave it two quick turns round his waist. He had no time to do more. The next instant he had been whipped off his perch and was being dragged through the water. But he clung to the rope with both hands, for he felt it was likely to cut him in halves unless something was soon done to relieve the strain.

What happened after that he didn't know. He never did know. All he knew was that he opened his eyes to find himself gasping like a stranded fish on the deck of the destroyer. Several sailors were looking at him curiously. Then an officer hurried forward and bent over him.

'Thanks,' he said. 'We got the case—and your message. But who the devil are you?'

Biggles saw that the officer was staring at his swastika armlet, which for the moment he had completely forgotten. 'Oh, that,' he laughed weakly. 'Don't take any notice of that. I'm a British agent. Take me to your skipper at once.'

Half supported by two sailors, for his legs were a bit groggy, he was taken to the bridge, where he was at once the cynosure of all eyes.

He looked at the captain. 'You got my message?'

'Yes—but who—'

Biggles broke in, and in a few crisp sentences told who he was, what he had done, and why he had done it. Naturally, he was able to go into more details than had been possible in the written message, with regard to the disposition of the enemy forces. 'If you shoot at the shore batteries, try not to hit the schoolhouse—it's full of British prisoners,' he concluded. 'Phew, I've had a hot five minutes.'

'Hot!' The captain permitted himself to smile. 'I'd call it something worse than that. It's likely to be hot on this ship, too, when we get round the next bend. You'd better get below.'

Biggles tried hard to think. Had it not been for Algy he would have been quite content to remain where he was, but he felt that somehow he ought to get back to the schoolhouse. Algy had come out to help him, so he could not leave him now.

'I've got to get back on shore,' he said at last.

The captain stared. Then he shrugged his shoulders. 'Well, you know your job,' he said simply. 'All I can say is I'd rather have my job than yours. I'm much obliged for the information. I'll remember it. By the way, what's your name?'

'Bigglesworth—Squadron Leader, R.A.F. If you get home safely you might notify Colonel Raymond of M.I.5. that you saw me. I won't waste any more of your time. I fancy the balloon is about to go up.* So long and good luck.'

Biggles left the bridge. He was determined to get ashore, but how this was to be done was not easy to see unless he swam for it, and the shore was nearly a quarter of a mile away. Normally he would be quite able to swim that distance, but he doubted his ability to do it in ice water, fully dressed; yet he could not discard his clothes. Still, he saw that he had just a chance. The Narvik fiord, like most fiords, was not straight; not only did it bend like a dog's leg, but there were places where cliffs jutted far out into the water. They had already passed one or two; another was just ahead, and Biggles saw that the captain had for some tactical reason altered his course to pass very close to it. Much as he disliked the idea, he decided that if the destroyer passed within a hundred yards of the rock he would go overboard. Beckoning to a chief petty officer who was standing near, he made him aware of his intention in order that it might not be thought that a man had accidentally fallen overboard. Then, standing tense, he waited for the crucial moment.

The rocky promontory, beyond which lay the town of Narvik, seemed to float nearer as the destroyer raced towards it. Beyond lay the enemy ships. Within a minute the battle would start. To his great satisfaction Biggles saw that the captain had edged even nearer to

*Slang: the battle is about to begin.

the rock than he had dared to hope. The intervening distance was not more than sixty yards or so. The time had come: it was now or never. Bracing himself, he took a running dive to get as far from the vessel as possible in order to clear the churning screws.

By the time he had come to the surface the destroyer's guns were roaring. The enemy ships had also opened fire and shells were dropping into the water. With his eyes on the rock, he put every ounce of strength he possessed into his stroke, and reached the point with greater ease than he had expected. Dragging himself ashore, he paused for a moment to wring as much water as possible out of his clothes, and then ran towards the town.

As he had hoped, he found everything in the wildest confusion, which was hardly to be wondered at, for until the German pilot reported their presence in the fiord, the arrival of the destroyers on the scene had not been expected. On the fiord itself a terrible battle was raging between eleven destroyers. Several German store-ships were also firing, and shore batteries added to the din. Nobody took the slightest notice of Biggles as he dashed towards the schoolhouse; indeed, very few people, either soldiers or civilians, were in sight. No doubt the troops were all at their stations, and the civilians had taken cover. The din was indescribable.

At the schoolhouse Biggles found a curious state of affairs. Only two elderly German soldiers remained on guard, and they were trying vainly to quieten the prisoners, who were cheering hysterically.

He went straight to the guards. 'Are the doors locked?' he asked tersely, indicating the schoolhouse.

'Yes.'

'Then I'll take charge here.' Biggles showed his Gestapo pass. It was wet, but that didn't matter. 'Give me the keys. You've got to get down to the shore,' he added. 'The British are going to land marines.'

The two soldiers did not question the order. There was no reason why they should, for it seemed highly probable that a landing would be attempted. Indeed, Biggles really hoped that a landing would be made. He watched the two Germans out of sight and then unlocked the school door. He was greeted with cheers, but by holding up his hands he managed to quell the clamour.

'You'll have to bolt for it,' he said. 'I can't do anything more for you. You'll have to take your chance. Get as far down the fiord as you can and hide. If our destroyers withdraw signal to them, and there is a chance that they may pick you up. That's all.'

The prisoners wasted no time. With the exception of Algy they made for the door.

'What had I better do?' asked Algy.

'You go with them.'

'And leave you here?'

'Yes, but only for the time being. I shall follow you,' said Biggles tersely. 'Believe me, I've had about enough of this. But it wouldn't do for us to be seen together. Where's Ginger?'

'He's somewhere off the coast in an aircraft carrier—at least, he ought to be. That's where I left him.'

'I see. We can't stop to talk now. You get along. I'll try to rejoin you outside the town. If the Boche see us together they'll guess what has happened. Cheerio—see you later.'

Algy dashed off after the sailors.

Biggles watched him go. He was by no means happy over the state of affairs. He would have much preferred to remain with Algy, but the reasons he had given for not doing so were genuine. If he was seen with the escapees the Germans would realize at once that he was not what he pretended to be. It was better that he should go alone. Later, perhaps, he would be able to join the fugitives and get away with them. He wished now that he had asked Algy a few questions about his movements, and about Ginger. The trouble was, the situation really demanded serious thought, but there had been little or no time to think. Things had happened—and were still happening—so fast that there was no time for lucid reasoning. Shells were now dropping into the town. Several buildings were alight and small parties of Germans were dashing about. A mighty cloud of smoke hung over everything, making it impossible to see what was happening on the fiord. Yet he felt he ought to know, for unless he knew who had won the battle he would not be able to judge if there was any chance of being picked up by one of the destroyers. Then, of course, there was always a chance that the British sailors would attack the town and capture it, in which case it would be safe for him to remain where he was. On the other hand, if the British destroyers were beaten off he would find himself isolated with the Germans. When things settled down there would be inquiries. The prisoners would be remembered, and if he were found going down the fiord it would look suspicious. In the end he decided that before doing anything else he would find out what was happening.

He went straight to the German head-quarters, and

was not questioned until he accidentally ran into the Commandant.

The Colonel frowned. 'I thought you had orders to get back to Boda?' he queried sharply.

'Quite right, sir,' returned Biggles evenly. 'Believe me, I wish I was on my way.'

'Why aren't you?'

'I started back in a 'plane, but by a bit of bad luck we were shot down by British anti-aircraft guns. We crashed in the fiord and I had to swim ashore. What is happening here?'

'The British are sinking our ships.'

'Will they try to land do you think?'

'No. I've just heard that they're going back down the fiord.'

At that moment a German pilot in Air Force uniform came running up. He saluted the Colonel.

'I'm getting away now, sir,' he said.

'Good.' The Commandant started. 'Just a minute. Have you got room for a passenger?'

'Certainly.'

The Colonel turned to Biggles. 'Here's your chance,' he declared. 'Schaffer is flying down to Oslo immediately. You can go with him and go on to Boda afterwards; you might not get another chance.'

'I can drop him at Boda if he likes,' offered Schaffer. 'I shall pass over the aerodrome on my way to Oslo.'

This didn't suit Biggles at all. He didn't want to go back down south, either to Boda or anywhere else. Now that he had learned that the British destroyers were going back down the fiord he wanted to rejoin Algy, get aboard one of them, and go back to England. But he daren't refuse the offer. All he could do was make excuses in the hope that Schaffer would go without him.

'I'm soaked to the skin,' he protested. 'I can't fly in these wet clothes—I shall be frozen stiff.'

'Don't worry about that,' put in Schaffer quickly, with irritating generosity. 'I can lend you some kit. My suitcase is in the machine; you can change in the cabin.'

'That's right,' cried the Commandant. 'You'd better obey your orders.'

Biggles saluted. 'Very good, sir.'

He followed Schaffer down to the wharf, to where a big flying-boat floated.

'You can't land me at Boda in a flying-boat,' Biggles pointed out.

Schaffer smiled condescendingly. 'She's an amphibian.'

'Ah! I understand.' A new hope sprang into Biggles' mind. Schaffer was unaware that he was a pilot, so he might overpower him in the air and take charge of the machine. If he could succeed in doing this he might fly straight on to England.

He followed Schaffer into the flying-boat, and his hopes instantly collapsed. There were already three German officers in it.

Schaffer pulled a suitcase off the rack. 'Here you are,' he said cheerfully. 'You'll find a spare uniform inside.' Then he went through to the cockpit.

In five minutes the flying-boat was in the air, heading south. Astern, from the fiord, a great pillar of smoke was rising.

# Chapter 7
# What Happened at Stavanger

It was late in the afternoon when Schaffer landed Biggles at Boda. He was still wearing the German's spare uniform, for his suit was not yet dry. He arranged with Schaffer that he would send the uniform on when his own things were dry, although as the German was by no means certain of his movements he would have to let Biggles know where to send them.

As soon as Biggles was on the ground, carrying his wet things in Schaffer's suitcase, the German pilot took off again, leaving Biggles standing on the aerodrome, now a scene of considerable activity.

Alert for danger, Biggles walked towards the officers' quarters. His position was, he knew, perilous in the extreme, but he couldn't remain standing on the aerodrome. What he feared was that he might run into Brandt, the man who knew him by sight. If von Stalhein happened to be with him, as seemed probable, then all deception would be at an end. All Biggles could do was mark down a Messerschmitt not far away, this offering the only possible means of escape if the worst came to the worst. To complicate matters, he would have to let von Hymann know that he was back, otherwise the Gestapo chief would start looking for him. He would learn that Schaffer had flown him back to Boda from Narvik, so should he, Biggles, fail to report, it would look most suspicious.

He dumped the suitcase in the room that had been allotted to him, and subjecting everyone he met to the closest scrutiny, he began making his way towards the station head-quarters. In doing so he met Kristen, who greeted him cordially but with surprise.

'Hello!' he cried. 'Where the deuce have you been?'

Biggles smiled ruefully. 'Don't talk about it,' he said sadly. 'I had to go up to Narvik on a special job. I was just starting for home, by air, when a flotilla of British destroyers arrived and we were shot down. We fell into the fiord, but I managed to swim ashore. *Himmel**! Was it cold!'

Kristen laughed. 'All in a day's work. Where are you bound for now?'

It struck Biggles as odd that Kristen did not mention his uniform. He wondered why.

'I'm just going to station head-quarters to report,' he answered. 'By the way, how do you like my uniform?'

'It fits badly. Also, I didn't know you had been promoted to *Oberleutnant*.'

'It isn't mine,' laughed Biggles. 'I got wet through, so these things were lent to me by a fellow named Schaffer—the chap who flew me back here.'

'I see. Some uniforms have now arrived here, so I thought, naturally, that you'd been and got yourself one. You can get one as soon as you like, but don't be too long or you may find them all gone. See you later.'

Biggles went on to head-quarters and reported to the Commandant, Baron von Leffers. He asked permission to use the telephone.

* German: heavens!

'Yes, you'd better report to von Hymann right away,' returned the Commandant sourly. 'There have been a lot of inquiries for you. Two fellows were here yesterday asking where you were.'

'What were their names?' inquired Biggles casually.

'Brandt and von Stalhein—a fellow in the Secret Service.'

Biggles nodded. 'I was expecting them,' he announced calmly, and put a call through to the Hotel Port.

In a minute he was speaking to von Hymann. Wasting no words, he reported that he was back at Boda, and was going on to report with more detail what had happened at Narvik when von Hymann stopped him.

'We know all about that,' said the Gestapo chief. 'After you had left I had a long talk with the Commander of the Narvik garrison, and he told me how Bigglesworth had got away—as he had learnt it from the British prisoners. Von Stalhein was very upset. He seems to hate this fellow Bigglesworth like poison, and he, too, had a long talk with Narvik. Pity this fellow Bigglesworth didn't remain with the party you captured, then we should have got him. Still, it's no use crying over split milk.'

Biggles's muscles tightened as his chief went on. 'Von Stalhein is here with me now. He says that this Bigglesworth is a tricky customer, so he wants all the particulars from you that he can get. He's coming along to see you.'

'When?'

There was a brief delay, presumably while the chief spoke to von Stalhein.

'Now,' answered von Hymann. 'He says he'll come

along right now. He'll be with you in less than an hour.'

It was the answer Biggles dreaded. 'Very good, sir.' Trying not to let his face reveal what he felt, he hung up the receiver.

'Everything all right?' inquired the Baron coldly.

'Right as rain,' returned Biggles.

Dusk was closing in as he left the office and started walking back towards his quarters. He had got to move quickly, that was certain. He had got to get away before von Stalhein arrived—but how? He felt that he was in a net, a net that was slowly but surely closing round him, and he could not even find respite, much less a way of escape.

So engrossed was he with his thoughts that he saw no one near him. He was hardly conscious of the light touch that fell on his arm. Something—it felt like a slip of paper—was pushed into his hand. Then the man was gone, faded into the shadows. Biggles caught no more than a glimpse of a grey uniform. He glanced around swiftly and then walked on slowly; and as he walked he unfolded the slip of paper. There was a message on it, printed in small block letters. It read:

'What is happening at Stavanger Airport? Particulars of planes and anti-aircraft defences urgently wanted. Also particulars of damage done. Get your report to Fiord 21, where messenger awaits you. If you are unable to land there, put message in a bottle and drop in fiord. R.'

Biggles memorized the message; then he put the slip in his mouth and chewed it to pulp. He could have laughed had his position not been so desperate. As if he hadn't got enough on his mind already! Now, in the middle of all his worries, was a message from Colonel Raymond, asking him to undertake a mission which bristled with difficulties. There was this about it though, he thought on reflection. His position was already so alarming that it could hardly be worse. Colonel Raymond, as promised, had got into touch with him. The man who had delivered the message, obviously a secret agent, must know him by sight—but (Biggles reasoned) he could have learned to recognize him from a photograph.

It gave him strength to know he was not alone within the enemy lines. Other men were doing the same thing. The fellow who had so cleverly slipped the paper into his hand was one of them. It was cleverly done because he had not even seen the man's face. He would not recognize him if he saw him, so he could never betray, either by accident or intentionally. They were all playing a dreadful game in which no one took a risk that could be avoided. He tore the chewed-up message to pieces and threw the pieces away.

Reaching the officers' mess, he stood still for a moment staring into the gathering gloom, trying to get his racing thoughts into some sort of order. Colonel Raymond's message was clear enough. He wanted him to go to Stavanger. Obviously he could not remain at Boda once von Stalhein had arrived on the scene, and since he had got to go somewhere, Stavanger suited him as well as anywhere. But after that he would not be able to return to Boda. Von Stalhein would be furious, not to say suspicious, when he arrived and found that the man whom he had come to see had gone off without leaving a message. What would von Stalhein do then? Biggles wondered. Most likely he would return to Oslo and voice his suspicions to von Hymann, who would start a hue and cry for him. Still, there was no way of preventing that. He couldn't let Colonel Raymond down. He would do his best to obtain the required information, and get it to Fiord 21. He knew the fiord well. Indeed, the number 21 was the one he himself had given it. It was one of the fiords he had marked down during his survey flights, and as it was a possible landing-place he had given particulars of it in the reports he had sent home. No doubt the Colonel had used the number, instead of the fiord's proper name, in order to convince him that the message was genuine. Further, should the message fall into wrong hands the recipient would not know to which fiord the number 21 referred. As far as Stavanger Airport was concerned, there was only one way he could get to it, and that was by air. The only aircraft available was a Messerschmitt—there were now several standing on the aerodrome. It meant flying in the dark, but he didn't mind that. The greatest danger would come when he tried to take the plane. However, he could but try.

Biggles went round to the back of the canteen, found a small empty bottle with a well-fitting cork and put it in his pocket. It was all the equipment he needed. He then returned to the aerodrome and reconnoitred the part where the planes were standing. Most of those which had been operating during the day had now returned, and were parked at intervals along the edge of the aerodrome—an anti-bombing precaution which suggested that a raid was feared. However, Biggles was not concerned with that. All he wanted was a machine, and as few people were about there did not appear to be any great difficulty in getting one. There might be an alarm when he took off, but by that time he would be in the air, so it wouldn't matter.

Unhurriedly, and without being accosted, he walked over to the nearest Messerschmitt and laid his hand on the engine cowling. It was still warm. A glance round revealed no sign of danger, so he climbed into the cockpit. Still no alarm was raised. He examined the instrument board carefully, and perceiving that the controls were of orthodox design, he decided to start. He had no flying kit, but that did not worry him; the journey, not more than a hundred miles, was too short for him to get really cold.

He wasted no more time. The engine spluttered as it sprang to life, and in another minute the machine was racing across the turf. He had taken off in the direction of his destination, so he could keep straight on towards the western coast, keeping low so that his identification markings could be seen easily if he were challenged. He was, many times. Searchlights leapt up along his line of flight, only to fade again as the operators found him and identified the aircraft for one of their own.

In less than half an hour he was gliding down through a perfect maze of searchlight beams that surrounded the airport of Stavanger. He made a mental note of the number of them, for they formed an important part of anti-aircraft equipment, about which Colonel Raymond was anxious to have particulars. Some of the beams followed him down, so as soon as the machine had finished its run he taxied straight on to the aerodrome buildings. A working-party under an N.C.O. ran out to meet him and to guide him in.

'I thought single-seaters were not to fly after dark unless there was a raid?' said the N.C.O.

This was evidently a new order, and Biggles knew nothing of it. 'Quite right,' he said smoothly. 'It happens, though, that the order does not apply to the special communication squadron to which I belong. I have a message for the Commandant.'

'Couldn't it have been telephoned, or radioed?' queried the N.C.O., who was evidently of an inquisitive nature.

'So that the enemy could pick it up, too?' sneered Biggles sarcastically. 'Not likely. Where is the Commandant's office?'

The N.C.O. pointed. 'Over there.'

'Thanks.'

Biggles walked on, leaving the working-party to continue its duties. He had no intention of seeking an interview with the Commandant. There was no reason why he should. He thought he could learn all there was to know about the place without asking pointed questions, either of the Commandant or anyone else. Which, in fact, he did. He went into the canteen, and, lingering over a coffee, listened to the conversations going on around him. After that he walked round outside, noting everything of interest—the number of machines, types, position of guns, &c. Only one man, a police corporal, challenged him, but the Gestapo pass worked as usual and the corporal said no more. Finally, Biggles returned to the canteen and, sitting quietly in a corner as though writing a letter, committed all the information he had gathered to writing. He was well aware of the danger of doing this, for should he for any reason be searched it would provide conclusive evidence against him. When it was done he returned to the aerodrome, and in the darkness inserted the paper into the bottle, afterwards corking it tightly.

Now all this had occupied more than an hour, and Biggles was just moving towards his machine with a view to going straight on to Fiord 21 when he became aware of a commotion. There was nothing definite about it; it took the form of a slightly increased activity. A messenger ran along the concrete apron in front of the hangars, shouting to another man. Small parties began to collect, talking excitedly. One such group stood near his machine. He walked quickly towards it but kept in the background.

'What's going on?' he asked a simple-looking soldier who stood near by.

'They say this machine was stolen from Boda,' was the startling reply.

'Stolen?'

'All I know is, a friend of mine in the orderly room told me that a message has just come through by telephone from Boda saying that someone had made off with the machine. They gave the number of it, and it has just been discovered that this is it. They're looking for the pilot who brought it here.'

Biggles did not doubt for one moment the truth of this alarming information. Nor did he waste time asking who was looking for the pilot. Obviously it would be fatal for him to go near the machine now. He would have to borrow another. Having reached that decision, he was turning away when there was a general stir. The searchlights switched on again, sweeping the heavens, whence came the noise of a gliding plane. A silver spark gleamed against the sky, and a minute or two later the machine, a two-seater, glided in and landed. As soon as it was on the ground it taxied quickly to where the Messerschmitt stood. A man jumped down, and Biggles had no need to look twice to see who it was. It was Erich von Stalhein. The German walked quickly towards the Commandant's office.

'It's getting time I was moving on,' Biggles told himself, and turned quickly towards the machines that lined the boundary of the aerodrome. In doing so he came face to face with a man whom he had no wish to see at that moment. It was the N.C.O. in charge of the working-party, the man who had accosted him on landing.

'Here! They're looking for you,' cried the N.C.O. sharply.

'Looking for me?' queried Biggles foolishly. 'Who's looking for me?'

'Everybody. You'd better come with me to the office and see the Commandant.'

Had the man been alone, Biggles might have been tempted to make a break for it, but during the conversation several soldiers and airmen had gathered round until he and the N.C.O. were in the centre of a circle. Nevertheless, he had not the slightest intention of walking unprotestingly to his doom—for that was what the Commandant's office amounted to now that von Stalhein was there. What he would have done had things remained normal will never be known. For once he was at a loss to know how to act for the best. And while he stood there staring at the N.C.O., trying to make up his mind, he heard a distant sound that set his pulses racing. It was the choking *whoof-whoof-whoof* of anti-aircraft gunfire, and it was drawing rapidly nearer.

'D'you know who I am?' Biggles asked the N.C.O., simply to gain time.

'Who are you?'

Biggles produced his Gestapo pass.

The corporal's manner changed; he became more respectful, but he did not retract. 'All the same, sir, I think you'd better report to the Commandant,' he insisted. 'There seems to be some trouble over your—'

The N.C.O. broke off, staring at the sky, while the soldiers and airmen dispersed like mist on a summer morning; for, from overhead, there came a sudden burst of aero engines. Apparently the machine, or machines, had been gliding. Almost simultaneously with the roar of the engines came an even more sinister sound. It was a shrill whine, increasing swiftly in volume until it sounded like the whistle of an express train.

The N.C.O. knew what it was. So did Biggles, for once heard there is no mistaking the sound of falling bombs. No longer concerned with Biggles, the N.C.O. ran for his life. Biggles, too, bolted, for he had an idea of what was going to happen to the aerodrome. From one point of view the British bombers had done him a good turn, but he had no desire to be blown to pieces by their bombs. He started to follow the N.C.O. and his men, assuming that they would know the nearest way to cover, but before he could overtake them the first bombs were bursting. The searchlights were raking the sky. Anti-aircraft guns roared. Bombs thundered. In short, pandemonium broke loose.

Biggles flung himself flat, his hands over his ears to prevent himself from being deafened. Bombs were falling all around. Some fell on the buildings and set fire to them, and in the lurid glare he could get a rough idea of the damage that was being done. The first wave of bombers passed, but he could hear more coming, and then, suddenly, he knew what they were doing. Apart from destroying the aerodrome buildings, they were churning the aerodrome itself into a sea of craters, thus putting it out of action.

Biggles caught his breath as he realized what this implied. If the bombers were going to make it impossible for machines to land, then they would also make it impossible for machines to take off, in which case he would be stranded at Stavanger—with von Stalhein. He perceived that if ever he was to get away it would have to be now, before any further damage was caused. Already it would be a risky business taking off, for if he got a machine and struck a crater while travelling at high speed, he would certainly break some bones. Furthermore, some of the machines were ablaze, and it seemed likely that they would set fire to the rest.

In a flash Biggles was on his feet, racing towards a machine which had so far escaped damage. He could hear another salvo of bombs coming down; guns flashed, and lines of tracer bullets streaked through the air. The noise was deafening. With one thing and another, he felt that he had suddenly gone mad in the middle of an inferno. There was this about it though, he thought, as he tore towards the machine: everyone would be too busy doing something, or taking cover, to pay any attention to him, even if he were seen.

Panting for breath, he reached the machine he had selected, and he laughed aloud when he recognized it for the one in which von Stalhein had arrived. Then he flung himself flat again as another lot of bombs rained down.

'Go to it boys!' he yelled, giving way to a fierce exultation as the bombs exploded. While the last report was still ringing in his ears he clambered into the machine.

In all his long flying career, with its many breathless incidents, he had never made a more fantastic take-off. Fantastic only half describes it. It was, he felt, the act of a madman—but then it would have been lunacy to remain.

To start with, it was neither light nor dark. It was both. Pitch darkness alternated with vivid flashes of blinding orange light as bombs exploded and guns flashed—not that it would have made much difference had the light been constant, for the aerodrome was now blanketed in a pall of smoke. As if this were not enough, several bombs had fallen on the landing field, leaving yawning craters.

For a moment, with his hand on the throttle, he blinked in a sort of daze through the windscreen, trying to make out something, anything, as long as it would give him a line to fly on, and help to keep him straight* But there was nothing—nothing but smoke. Again, the noise was indescribable, and sufficient in itself to prevent coherent thought.

In sheer desperation Biggles jerked the throttle open, and in a moment was tearing blindly through the turmoil. There then followed twenty seconds of such strain that his nerves seemed to be stretched like elastic; but at the end of that brief period of time—which, in fact,

* In taking off a pilot chooses a mark, usually on the boundary of the aerodrome, to prevent swerving.

seemed longer than the bare figure suggests—he could tell by the 'feel' of the controls that the machine was ready to lift. He eased the joystick back. Instantly the cessation of vibration, caused by the wheels running over the ground, told him that he was air-borne. He could still see nothing, but as he climbed the smoke thinned, and a vague misty world began to take shape around him.

The first substantial object that he saw was another machine coming straight towards him, and only by a spasmodic jerk of the controls did he avoid a head-on collision. As the other machine flashed past he made out the dim silhouette of a Blenheim. Dry-lipped with strain, he held the stick forward for a moment or two and then zoomed high into a blue-black world torn by jabbing flame and hurtling metal. Below, the aerodrome was an inferno. The risk of collision with the British bombers or of flying into the bombs that were raining down was still imminent, but he could do no more than hold on a steady course and hope for the best. Another anxious minute passed, each second of it reducing the risk, and then his taut nerves began to relax.

'Holy smoke! What a picnic,' he gasped, and then swung round to the north towards Fiord 21. He could see the sea below him now and the deeply indented coast-line, so his immediate mission became nothing more difficult than straight-forward flying, or so he thought.

His destination lay about fifty miles away, and he had covered half that distance in a few minutes when he detected a faint reek of petrol. He was unable to see anything, so he could only feel about with his hand,

and in doing so he made the disconcerting discovery that the floor of his cockpit was wet with petrol. He guessed what had happened. Either while the machine had been standing on the ground, or after it was in the air, it had been hit by a piece of shrapnel, and the tank had been holed. There was nothing he could do about it, of course, except switch on the instrument-board light and look at the petrol gauge. One glance told him the worst. The tank was practically empty. He at once looked at his altimeter, which told him that he had climbed to four thousand feet. That gave him a chance. If only the engine would hold out for another five minutes he would be within gliding distance of the fiord.

It did — nearly. He could see the fiord in the distance, for he had flown over the district several times for the purpose of making his reports, and had it not been for this he would have been in a worse case than he was. He was still by no means certain that he would reach the fiord, but he could only hold on in an endeavour to do so. He switched off the ignition, for the engine was back-firing, and anyway it could serve no useful purpose. In dead silence he glided on towards the fiord, losing height slowly but steadily. And as he glided he made up his mind what he would do when he reached the water. Not that there was really any choice, for the aircraft was a land machine, without any adaptations for landing on water. This at once meant that he would have to pancake* on the surface of the fiord, for a landing on the jagged rocks that surrounded it was out of the question. Still, he thought that with judgement,

* A landing where, instead of the aircraft gliding down to land, it flops down from a height of a few feet after losing flying speed.

and a little luck, the machine would remain afloat until—until what? He wondered. Someone would be there waiting for him—or at any rate for the bottled message. It seemed unlikely that Colonel Raymond would order a message to be dropped into the fiord unless he was positive that someone would be there to collect it. Indeed, his message said that someone would be there. In that case he, Biggles, would be picked up. If there was no one there, then he would have to swim ashore, and with the possibility of this in view he decided to pancake as near the rocks as possible.

And that is what he did. Skimming the towering cliffs that bordered the fiord with only a few feet to spare, Biggles turned up the long narrow stretch of water, losing height, and keeping as near to the cliffs as he dared. He knew that a short distance ahead this cliff had partly collapsed in a mighty landslide, and this, if he could reach it, would provide the easiest place to get ashore.

As soon as the landslide came into view he side-slipped steeply to lose height. Ten feet above the surface of the black water he flattened out, and as the controls began to go 'sloppy', telling him that the machine was about to fall out of his hands, he kicked the rudder hard to bring the nose towards the sloping mass of boulders that thrust outward like a promontory and ended at the water's edge.

He was well satisfied with his landing. There was a terrific splash as the aircraft flopped bodily on to the water, but it floated, and surged forward to within a few yards of the rocks. By climbing along the wing he would be able to jump ashore, which pleased him immensely, for he fully expected a ducking, and the idea of spending the rest of the night in wet clothes was not pleasant to think about. He was kneeling on the centre section preparatory to climbing along the wing to the shore when a voice spoke.

'D'you always land like that?' asked someone evenly, in English.

Biggles nearly fell into the water. His hand flew to his gun, and half drew it. Then he stopped dead, staring. Slowly he pushed the pistol back into his pocket.

'Christopher Columbus!' he gasped. 'Ginger! How in the name of all that's miraculous did *you* get here?'

Ginger stood on a rock with his hands thrust deep into his trousers' pockets. 'I shouldn't call it a miracle,' he answered calmly. 'Raymond sent me along to meet you. Mind you don't slip—the water's colder than the tip of an Eskimo's nose.'

# Chapter 8
# Explanations and Decisions

Biggles scrambled ashore. He was just in time to escape a ducking, for the aircraft was sinking fast.

'How long have you been here?' he asked.

'Since last night.'

'Great Scott! You must be hungry.'

'Not me,' grinned Ginger. 'For all I knew it might have been a week before you turned up, so I brought some grub along.'

'Lead me to it,' returned Biggles promptly. 'I need some nourishment. We can talk as we eat—and there seems to be a lot to say. I assume you've got a machine here?'

'Of course.'

'Thank goodness for that. After we've eaten we'll push off home—and I don't mind telling you I shall be mighty glad to get out of this.'

Ginger looked up sharply. 'Home?'

'Of course—why not?'

'But what about Algy?'

'What about him?'

'He's gone to Boda.'

Biggles swayed. Then he sank down on a rock. For a moment or two he was speechless. 'Gone to Boda?' he managed to get out. 'What in heaven's name for?'

'To find you.'

Biggles shook his head sadly. 'Get the grub,' he said wearily. 'It's time we got this straightened out.'

Ginger led the way to a tiny cove where, under an overhanging cliff, a seaplane rested on the water. From behind a rock he produced a heavy bag. 'Help yourself,' he said, dropping the bag in front of Biggles. 'There's bread, cheese, sardines, and a flask of cold tea. That's all I could manage.'

'That'll suit me,' Biggles assured him. 'Now let's try to untangle things. I'll start. I got a message from Raymond asking me to get information about Stavanger and bring it here. I was told if necessary to drop the information in a bottle. Instead, I dropped myself— I'll tell you why presently. The bottle is still in my pocket. I've got the information and we've got to get it to Raymond. That's all I have to say except that the last time I saw Algy he was a prisoner at Narvik. I helped him to get away—at least, I hoped he'd got away.'

Ginger nodded. 'That's right, he did.'

'Before we go any farther, d'you reckon this is a safe spot?' inquired Biggles.

'I should say not; but nowhere in Norway is safe, and this is as good as anywhere. We can't be seen— except, of course, by a vessel coming up the fiord, and only then in daylight.'

'Good. Now tell me about Algy.'

'Well, what happened was this,' explained Ginger. 'To start with, Colonel Raymond brought us back home from France; he told us what you'd been doing and how you were fixed. I may say we were both pretty fed up about it, but that didn't cut any ice. Naturally, we felt that we ought to be helping, but it wasn't easy to see what we could do, or how we could get into touch with you. Raymond soon fixed things up though. He said a British force was on its way to Norway, but he wasn't allowed to tell us where the landings would be made. The force would be supported by the Navy, and machines of the Fleet Air Arm, which would operate chiefly from aircraft carriers. Raymond was able to arrange for us to fly out to a carrier; he told us to keep an eye on Narvik, as if possible he would get a message through to you asking you to fly up to Narvik Fiord. If you could then make a smoke signal we might be able to pick you up. I must say it seemed a pretty wild hope, but it was all Raymond could do.'

'I didn't get any message asking me to go to Narvik,' put in Biggles.

'We suspected that—in fact, we knew it, because the agent sent a signal back to Raymond to say that you'd left Boda. At least, he couldn't find you there. Obviously, if the fellow couldn't get into touch with you he couldn't give you the message.'

'True enough,' agreed Biggles.

'Well, we joined the carrier off the coast of Norway,' continued Ginger. 'We were flown out, but being supernumeraries we couldn't get machines of our own; consequently we could only get trips in other fellows' machines. I did a trip, but saw nothing. Mind you, we were still hoping that the agent would find you and send you up. Algy then went off straight away as a gunner in a Shark. It got its engine shot up and was forced to land on the fiord. That's how he came to be taken prisoner. Naturally, I didn't know anything about it at the time. All I knew was that the Shark failed to return, and I reckoned poor old Algy was a goner. Dash my wig if he didn't turn up with a tale that I found pretty hard to swallow.'

'You mean—he got back to the carrier?'

'Yes, he was picked up by a destroyer. He told me a fantastic tale about being taken prisoner, and with some other fellows being shoved into the schoolhouse at Narvik. Then who should blow along, as large as life but you, acting as though you'd bought the whole outfit. You inspected the prisoners and went off again. Shortly afterwards our destroyers barged into the fiord and had a crack at the enemy. Upon this you came back and set the prisoners free. Algy said he kept with the crowd, expecting you to follow, but he didn't see you again. He didn't know what your game was, so when our destroyers steamed out, and the party had a chance of being picked up, he went aboard with the rest. There were three fellows off the carrier among the prisoners, so the destroyer dumped them back on board. That's how Algy got back, and how I learnt all about this.'

'What happened next?'

'Well, we didn't know what to do for the best, and we were still scratching our heads when Raymond got another message through to us. He said his man was still trying to make contact with you at Boda, because he felt certain that you'd return there sooner or later. If the agent did make contact with you he was to ask you to go to Stavanger and collect information, and then come on here, to Fiord 21. Raymond suggested that we should get an aircraft and come down here to wait for you. If you turned up we were to fly you home.'

'That sounds as if Raymond has given me permission to leave the country.'

'That's pretty obvious.'

'But how did Algy—'

'Just a minute—I'm coming to that. There was a snag, and it was this. There was no great difficulty in our flying down here, but we didn't know, and had no means of finding out, if you'd got the message asking you to come here. If you *hadn't* got the message, then we might have sat here for the duration waiting for you. The result was that Algy, who knew you must be in a pretty tight spot and anxious to get away, got one of his bright ideas. It was that he should go to Boda to find you, and so make certain of getting you here.'

'But how the dickens did he propose getting to Boda?'

'His idea was to get one of the fellows on the carrier to fly him over, at night. He would step out with his parachute.'

Biggles stared aghast. 'But he must have been crazy!'

Ginger shrugged his shoulders. 'He always was, wasn't he?'

'And d'you mean to tell me that's what he did?'

'That, chief, is what he did.'

'But surely not in his own uniform?'

'More or less. He'd picked up a German great-coat from somewhere, and he simply wore that over his uniform. The last I saw of him he was getting into the machine, bound for Boda. I was to come here and wait, and here I am.'

'And you don't know what's happened to Algy?'

'Absolutely nothing. I haven't heard a word since he took off. Of course, I hoped you'd arrive together.'

Biggles squatted on the rock with his chin in the palms of his hands. 'Well, this is a pretty kettle of fish,

I must say,' he muttered. 'Here am I, at last able to get out, only to find that Algy has got himself stuck inside.'

'When he finds you're not at Boda he may be able to grab a machine and fly here.'

Biggles snorted. 'Suffering crocodiles! Is he daft enough to think that the Boche leave their machines lying about for anybody to pick up?'

'You seem to have managed it.'

'That's different. I'm an officer in the German Air Force. If that isn't enough I'm also a member of the Gestapo, with a special pass, signed by the chief, in my pocket. It wasn't hard for me to move about, although it was a bit risky because von Stalhein is in Norway looking for me. By a bit of bad luck it was learned that I was in Norway.'

Biggles gave a brief account of his adventures. 'So you see,' he concluded, 'it was a lot easier for me to get a machine than it will be for Algy. If he's in Boda, then I reckon he's stuck there.'

Ginger stared moodily at the sombre surface of the fiord. 'In that case the question is, what are we going to do about it?'

Biggles thought for a moment. 'The most important thing of all is to get this information about Stavanger back to Colonel Raymond,' he decided. 'We can't allow personal matters to interfere with our Service jobs. You'd better take this information back. Raymond will be expecting it.'

'What about you?'

'I shall have to stay here to see if Algy turns up. If he does, we'll both be here when you return, so you'll be able to pick us both up. You can leave the food here with me. What's the time?' Biggles looked at his watch. 'It's nearly midnight—let's see—it's nearly four hundred and fifty miles across the ditch—call it three hours. If you spend an hour with Raymond—no, I'm afraid you couldn't get back here before daylight.'

'What's the matter with coming back after daylight?'

Biggles shook his head. 'Too risky. There are too many eyes along the coast right now. It would be much safer to slip in after dark. You could cut your engine well out to sea and glide in.'

'But that would mean you'd be here all day to-morrow.'

'That can't be prevented.'

'What about Algy?—I'm worried about him.'

'Let's leave it like this,' suggested Biggles. 'You get the information home—I've got it written out. You can also tell the Colonel what I've told you. I'll wait here for Algy; otherwise, if he came back and found no one here, he'd wonder what had happened. When you come back bring a spare parachute. If Algy hasn't turned up then you'll have to fly me over to Boda. I'll drop off and look for him. You could then fly back here and wait.'

'Okay,' agreed Ginger, 'but I'm bound to say it sounds a sticky business to me,' he added glumly.

'All war is sticky business,' Biggles reminded him. 'Get off now and concentrate on getting home. That should give you plenty to think about without worrying about me.'

Ginger cast off the mooring rope that held his machine close against the rocks and climbed into the cockpit. Biggles, putting his hands on a float, pushed the machine clear. For a few moments a brooding hush reigned, a hush broken only by the gentle lap of the dark water. Then the engine shattered the silence. The aircraft surged down the fiord and disappeared into the gloom.

Biggles put the food behind a rock and settled down to wait. From far away came the deep rumble of guns, but in the little fiord all was quiet. Nothing moved.

# Chapter 9
# Back at Boda

Algy did not come.

All through the long night hours Biggles waited, listening, hoping, for he had no wish to return to Boda. Several times he sat up, alert, as he heard the purr of aircraft. But they were only patrols—British or German, he knew not which—exploring the starlit heavens. Each time the sound died away he sank back again to wait. There was nothing he could do.

Dawn came, and with it still more aircraft, always flying very high. Only one, a German reconnaissance plane, came low over the silent fiord. Biggles took cover, and presently, apparently satisfied that the fiord was deserted, the German passed on. Occasionally Biggles ate a little of the food from the bag, but he ate mechanically and without relish, for he was too concerned with the state of affairs. The day wore on. The sun went down. Purple twilight, ever darkening, hung for a little while over the silent waters, and then gave way to night. Stars appeared, twinkling. Biggles munched a biscuit thoughtfully.

It was about half-past nine that he heard the sound for which he had been waiting, the musical hum of a gliding plane, and presently he saw its dark silhouette dropping slowly towards the water. There was a surging splash as it struck the surface and forged on towards the promontory formed by the landslide. Slowly it came to rest, and Ginger's head appeared. He gave a low whistle.

Biggles answered and, reaching out, caught a float to steady the machine.

'Everything all right?' inquired Ginger.

'Yes, nothing's happened here.'

'Did Algy come?'

'No.'

'Then it looks as if he's in a jam.'

'I'm afraid so. How did you get on? Any trouble?'

'Nothing to speak of. I ran into a Hun over the North Sea, but I managed to lose him. I saw Raymond and told him how things stood here. He was in favour of your flying straight back home.'

'But what about Algy?'

'He said he'd try to arrange for one of his agents in the country to pick him up and get him across the frontier into Sweden.'

Biggles shook his head. 'That won't do. Raymond ought to know we don't work like that. While Algy's inside the country I'm not going to leave it.'

'As a matter of fact, I think Raymond knew you'd take that attitude, and merely made his suggestion to let you know that if you wanted to come home he wouldn't object. What are you going to do?'

'It's no use my sitting here any longer. I doubt if Algy will come now. I shall have to go to Boda to fetch him. You've got a brolly*?'

'Yes.'

'Then you can take me over to Boda right away.'

Ginger, who by this time had come ashore, looked glum. 'I don't like it,' he muttered. 'It would be safer

* Slang: parachute.

for you to go and sit on the edge of a volcano than go to Boda. What are you going to say when they ask you why you pinched that Messerschmitt?'

'They don't know definitely that it was me.'

'They'll assume it was, I bet. They are certain to ask you about it.'

'I shall have the answers ready.'

'What about von Stalhein? I know you last saw him at Stavanger, but he may have gone back to Boda.'

Biggles shrugged his shoulders. 'That's a risk I shall have to take. I'll keep my eyes open.'

'You haven't forgotten that von Stalhein knows Algy? If he spotted him and has had him arrested, he'll be waiting for you to arrive. He knows by now that if he finds one of us it's only a question of time before the others turn up. I—'

'It's no use raising objections,' broke in Biggles impatiently. 'Whether he's got Algy or not, I'm going over to look for him. I've still got my Gestapo pass. After I drop off you come back here and wait; but if anyone spots you you'd better see about saving yourself.'

Ginger nodded.

'Then let's get away.'

Biggles donned the parachute, adjusted the harness, and took his place in the spare seat.

'You know better than I do where the aerodrome is, so keep me on my course if I look like going astray,' said Ginger as he got into the cockpit. 'I expect we shall get a good plastering from flak*.'

'Head out to sea first and get plenty of height,'

* Anti-aircraft fire.

advised Biggles. 'Switch off your engine when I tell you, and glide.'

'Will the aerodrome be blacked out?'

'I expect so, but I know too well where it is to have any difficulty in finding it. Go ahead.'

In a few minutes they were in the air, standing out to sea, climbing steadily for height. Not until they were at fifteen thousand feet did Ginger turn and head back towards the questing searchlight beams that marked the positions of enemy forces. These positions were avoided as far as possible, but more than once a beam leapt up and passed close enough to the machine to reflect on it a ghostly radiance. On such occasions Ginger throttled back and employed such ruses as Biggles had taught him.

'You're getting a little too far north,' Biggles said once, and that was the only remark he made until they were nearing their objective, when he gave more detailed instructions. They were now at twenty thousand feet.

'Hold her as she is and you'll pass right over the aerodrome,' he said finally. 'As soon as you feel me go off get back to the fiord. After that you'll have to use your discretion. Well, here we go.'

'S'long chief,' called Ginger huskily.

'S'long, laddie.' The machine rocked as Biggles dived overboard.

Ginger instinctively looked down, but he could see nothing except the inevitable searchlight beams that were still seeking him. It was with a heavy heart that he turned back towards the coast.

Biggles was still falling through the war-stricken sky. He had deliberately delayed pulling the ripcord for several seconds, but when he did so, and the fabric ballooned out above him, he gazed down at the darkened earth beneath. He could see the aerodrome now, and was satisfied that his jump had been well timed; he would touch down not more than a few hundred yards to the east of it.

He fell when he landed, but he was on his feet in a moment. He could still hear the drone of Ginger's machine fading away to the west, otherwise all was silent. Working quickly, he folded the parachute into a ball and looked round for a place to hide it. There appeared to be only one, and that was a ditch. There was water in the bottom of it, and into this he thrust the parachute and trod on it. This done, he made his way towards the aerodrome, aware that he was taking the most appalling risk he had ever willingly undertaken, a risk compared with which his original task was as nothing. If von Stalhein had returned to Boda, then he was virtually committing suicide.

Nobody challenged him as he walked towards his quarters, for this, he decided, might be the safest place for him until he had made certain inquiries that he had in mind, inquiries concerning Algy and von Stalhein. Near the officers' mess he met a German whom he knew slightly, and he was about to accost him when Kristen appeared. Kristen stopped dead when he saw Biggles.

'Where have you come from?' he demanded in an amazed voice.

'What do you mean—where have I come from?' returned Biggles.

'Where were you all day yesterday?'

'I've been doing a job for the Gestapo—I thought I told you that?'

'Yes, you did, but—well, I thought—people have been looking for you.'

'People? For me? Why?' Biggles feigned bland surprise.

'But wasn't it you who took the machine from here, the Messerschmitt, and made off with it?'

'Machine? What on earth are you talking about?'

'Somebody took a Messerschmitt from here without permission, and as you couldn't be found it was thought that you had taken it. A fellow named von Stalhein was here looking for you. The word came that the missing machine had landed at Stavanger, so he went on there.'

'Then I'd better have a word with him—that is, if he is back here,' said Biggles calmly. 'D'you happen to know if he came back?'

'He may have done, but I haven't seen him.'

'Then I'll ring up my chief in Oslo and find out.'

Biggles moved on towards the orderly room, but stopped suddenly. 'By the way, what is this rumour I hear about an English spy being captured here?'

Kristen shook his head. 'I haven't heard anything about it. What did you hear?'

'Only that a strange Englishman had been found prowling about the aerodrome.'

'Well, I've heard nothing of it.'

Biggles nodded. 'Evidently it was only a rumour— see you later.' He walked on, well satisfied with his inquiries.

While it was by no means certain, he thought, it rather looked as if von Stalhein had not come back to

Boda; and it was hardly likely that Algy had been captured without Kristen hearing something about it. It might be assumed, then, that Algy was still at large, and since his mission was to find Biggles, it was reasonable to suppose that he would be near the aerodrome— if not actually on it. But where? Where could he be?

Biggles tried to put himself in Algy's place, asking himself how he would have acted had the position been reversed. The most reasonable supposition, he concluded, was that Algy would not actually be on the aerodrome, where he would be open to question, but was more likely to be hiding near the boundary, watching and waiting for a chance to speak to him. In the circumstances Biggles thought he might take a walk round the aerodrome boundary, whistling a tune known to both of them; then, if Algy were near, he would reveal himself. But there was something he would have to do first, and that was to endeavour to allay suspicions concerning himself. The best way of doing that might be to ring up the Hotel Port and speak to von Hymann. He could tell him that he had been looking for von Stalhein.

With this object in view he made his way to the squadron office where, finding the adjutant* in charge, he asked permission to use the telephone for the purpose of getting into touch with von Hymann at the Hotel Port. Permission was given, but not until he had been subjected to a further difficult cross-examination, for it seemed that the adjutant was also under the impression that it was he who had taken the Messerchmitt. However, Biggles satisfied him by referring

* Officer appointed to assist the Commanding Officer with correspondence and paperwork.

vaguely to his Gestapo duties, and put the call through to von Hymann.

It was answered by von Stalhein. He announced his name.

Even before his crisp 'Hello' had faded from the wire Biggles knew that he had made a blunder. Not so much a blunder, perhaps, as an error of judgement. He felt that he should have thought of the possibility of von Stalhein answering the telephone, since, after the bombing of Stavanger, Oslo was the most likely place for him to go to; and in Oslo he would certainly make for Gestapo head-quarters.

Biggles realized this now, but up to that moment the possibility had not dawned on him. However, he did not lose his head. He could not afford to do so, for the adjutant was watching him curiously. And for this same reason he dare not dissemble by giving a fictitious name. All he dare do was alter his tone of voice, for unless he did so von Stalhein would recognize it at once. He might do so, anyway.

'This is number 2001,' said Biggles; 'I wish to speak to Oberleutnant von Hymann.'

'Von Hymann is not here. I am answering for him,' returned von Stalhein curtly. 'What did you say your number was?'

'2001.'

There was a brief pause. Then, 'What is your name?' asked von Stalhein.

'My orders were to use a number only, sir.'

'I am now asking you for your name. What is it?'

'Hendrik—Leutnant Hendrik.' Biggles could almost see von Stalhein's face at the other end of the line.

There was another short pause. 'What game d'you

think you're playing? You know I've been looking for you?'

'So I understand, sir, but it seems that we have just missed each other. I was given a job to do by Oberleutnant von Hymann.'

'Where are you speaking from now?'

'From Boda.'

Another pause. 'Indeed! Well, I want to see you, to get details of your adventure in Narvik.'

'You mean about the English spy, Bigglesworth?'

'Yes.' Von Stalhein's voice was little more than a whisper.

'Would you like me to proceed further with the—'

'No,' interrupted von Stalhein sharply. 'Remain where you are.'

'I'll come to Oslo and report to you if you wish,' offered Biggles, to gain time.

'No, I'd rather come out to Boda. On no account leave the aerodrome until I arrive.'

'Can I expect you—to-night?'

There was yet another pause. 'No, I'm too busy here to leave just now. I'll be along in the morning,' said von Stalhein casually.

'Then I'll wait for you here. Good-night, sir.'

Biggles hung up, thinking fast. He knew that both he and von Stalhein had been bluffing. No doubt the German had been as taken aback by the call as he had been to hear him answer it. Both had fenced—neither of them could very well do anything else.

'I gather you're not very popular at the moment,' said the German.

Biggles grimaced. 'It isn't my fault. I wasn't attached to the Gestapo from choice. I'm a pilot. Frankly, the sooner I've finished with this Gestapo business and get on regular flying work the better I shall be pleased.'

The adjutant seemed inclined to be sympathetic. Like most German soldiers he had no love for the Gestapo. 'I'll see what I can do about it,' he promised. 'Meanwhile, don't leave the aerodrome.'

'Of course not,' agreed Biggles, and went out.

But he did not go far. He had a suspicion. Whether von Stalhein had recognized his voice or not he did not know, but in any case he would be very, very anxious to see this elusive Norwegian named Hendrik—too anxious to wait until the morning. Biggles knew von Stalhein too well to suppose that he would delay his visit for several hours—time for him to get away. No! It was quite possible that von Stalhein had said that he would not be along that night in order to lull him into a false sense of security. It was far more likely that he would start for Boda forthwith in a fast car.

A minute later Biggles heard the sound he expected to hear. It was the shrill jangle of the telephone. Standing close to the door he thought straining his ears he could hear the adjutant's end of the conversation.

'You mean Hendrik, sir?' he was saying. 'Yes, he's still on the aerodrome.'

Biggles smiled grimly.

'Did you say arrest him?' continued the adjutant in a surprised voice. 'Of course, sir, if you say so. What is the charge? Leave it until you come—very well, sir. I'll have Hendrik watched, and if he attempts to leave the aerodrome I'll have him arrested immediately. You'll be along in—half an hour. Very good, sir.' There was a clang as the adjutant hung up the receiver.

Biggles waiting for no more. With the adjutant about

to detail men to watch him, and von Stalhein due to arrive in half an hour, he felt that Boda, from being unhealthy, had become malignant. He walked briskly away into the moonlight, realizing that he was now virtually a fugitive, yet forbidden by his code of honour even to attempt to escape while Algy was there looking for him. Where was Algy?

In sheer desperation Biggles began walking along the boundary of the aerodrome, whistling quietly, aware that now people on the aerodrome were looking for him the very minutes of his freedom were numbered. He broke into a run, and finally, in sheer desperation, called Algy by name. But there was no reply. Sick at heart he hurried on and completed a circuit of the aerodrome. Looking at his watch he saw that half an hour had elapsed since von Stalhein had rung up. The moon was now high, making it dangerous for him to move about.

Despondent, and hardly knowing what to do next, he made his way to the hangars, taking care to keep within their deepest shadows. Watching, he saw a car coming up the private drive that led from the main road to the club-house. Outside the orderly room, which was less than a hundred yards from where he stood, it stopped. A slim figure alighted and moved quickly. It was von Stalhein.

Biggles watched him for a moment with a peculiar smile on his face; then he walked quickly towards the main road. He felt that whatever Algy's predicament might be, no useful purpose could be served by remaining where he was. He could not stay at Boda. If he did, capture was inevitable, and once that happened all hope of helping Algy—or himself for that matter—

117

would be gone. While he remained at large there was still a chance—not a very bright one, admittedly, but a slim chance is better than none at all.

Now in order to reach the main road it was necessary for him to walk across the open moonlit area traversed by the drive. There were no trees, no bushes, nothing to offer cover, for these, as is customary near aerodromes, had been removed to prevent them from becoming obstructions to the movement of aircraft. He had gone only a few yards when there was a shout behind him. Looking back he saw Kristen, running, followed by a car—von Stalhein's car.

Kristen shouted. 'Hi! Stop! They want you in the office.'

'You're telling me,' muttered Biggles grimly.

He could, he thought, outrun Kristen, but there could be no escape from the car, which had now increased its speed and was fast overtaking him. Seeing that flight could no longer avail him, he drew his pistol and waited. He was in no mood to face von Stalhein's triumph.

As the car drew level a head appeared at the window, and he saw that the driver wore a German uniform greatcoat.

'Can I give you a lift?' said a calm voice, in English.

For a split second Biggles stood transfixed, his lips parted, his expression almost one of idiocy. Then he gulped, and flung himself into the car.

The driver was Algy.

'Where would you like to go, sir?' he inquired whimsically, after the manner of a taxi-driver.

'Anywhere,' gasped Biggles, 'but get going and make it fast.'

'Certainly, sir.' Algy swung into the main road and pressed the accelerator flat.

# Chapter 10
# On the Run

For perhaps a minute neither Biggles nor Algy spoke. As a matter of fact it took Biggles that time to recover from the shock. Then, 'where the dickens did you spring from?' he inquired.

'Oh, I was just hanging around, you know, in case I was wanted,' returned Algy lightly.

'Where did you get that uniform?'

'It's only a greatcoat. I borrowed it from the souvenir chest of the ship I was in.'

'Oh, yes—I remember now; Ginger told me about it,' nodded Biggles. 'Where did you get this car?'

'It was standing outside station head-quarters.'

'You know to whom it belongs?'

'Too true I do. I saw von Stalhein get out.'

Biggles laughed hysterically. 'Strewth! Last night I pinched his plane; now we've got his car. We shall have to drop him a line and thank him for providing us with transport.'

'As a matter of fact,' continued Algy, 'I was hanging around near head-quarters hoping to see you—which I did. I saw you break cover and make for the road, and it was obvious that you were in a tight spot. Von Stalhein's car was standing where he had left it, so, knowing how you hate walking, I thought I might as well bring it along.'

'Thanks, laddie,' said Biggles seriously. 'You were

just about in time. Things were getting hot—too jolly hot.'

Algy grinned. 'So I gathered. But isn't it time we decided where to go?'

'Ginger's waiting for us in the fiord,' declared Biggles. 'We ought to try to get to him, but I'm afraid we should never get there in this car. Von Stalhein will get on the phone and warn his patrols to be on the look-out for us. Of course, it would take a bit of time to warn everybody, so there's a chance that we might reach Oslo. If we go on at this rate we ought to do it in twenty minutes, and that will hardly be long enough for von Stalhein's crowd to get barricades up. Make for Oslo.'

'And then what?'

'Let's wait until we get there before we decide that. We may have to leave the car and hide, and hiding will be easier in a city than in open country. We'll make for the harbour. There were some flying-boats there the last time I saw the place. For your information, I'm a member of the Gestapo; I mention that because I've got a pass in my pocket which may help us.'

'Will it still work, do you think?' queried Algy. 'Won't von Stalhein take steps to have the bearer of it arrested?'

'Unquestionably; but with the country in this state it will take him a but of time to notify every German in Norway. Speed now is everything.'

'So you've seen Ginger? What had he got to talk about?'

'He gave me the low-down on everything. Afterwards I sent him to England with some information, and when he came back he brought me over to Boda. He should be back at the fiord now. Unfortunately I got there too late to stop you coming to look for me. Incidentally, in the information I sent back to Raymond I told him about Boda, and suggested that our bombers came over and knocked the place about a bit. That was one of the reasons why I was in a hurry to get you out of it.'

'This may be our boys coming now,' put in Algy, peering upwards through the windscreen.

Looking through the window, Biggles saw that the sky was ablaze with searchlights. At a terrific height specks of flame marked the burst of anti-aircraft gun-fire.

'By Jingo! You're right! Those are our fellows,' declared Biggles. 'They've come at a good moment. When they start dropping their loads on the aerodrome the people there will have something else to think of besides telephoning to Oslo about us.'

'I hope a bomb lands rights in von Stalhein's lap,' muttered Algy vindictively.

'That would be a pity,' protested Biggles reproachfully. 'It would take half the interest out of life.'

'It would make life a thundering sight easier,' snorted Algy. 'I'm all for a quiet life, and this is not my idea of it.'

'By gosh! Look at that flak!' broke in Biggles. 'There's a chance that when von Stalhein tried to get through to Oslo he found all the wires engaged, giving air-raid warnings. Hullo! There goes the first crump*,' he went on quickly as the flash of an exploding bomb lit up the sky.

* Sound of a bursting bomb.

'Shall we stop and watch the raid?' suggested Algy.

'Not on your life. I was caught in one at Stavanger last night, and that will last me for a long time. Let's push on to Oslo.'

As they sped down the road Biggles gave Algy a brief account of his adventures since he last saw him at Narvik, and Algy described his, although having talked to Ginger, there was little that Biggles did not know.

By the time these notes had been exchanged they were running through the suburbs of Oslo. They were stopped only once, at a cross-roads, but the Gestapo pass worked as usual. Whether von Stalhein had been unable to get through to Oslo on the telephone, or whether his conversation, or the subsequent arrangements, had been upset by the raid, they did not know, but it was evident that the patrol knew nothing about the car being taken. As far as the occupants were concerned, as both were—or appeared to be—in German uniforms, there was nothing in their appearance to arouse suspicion.

Biggles guided Algy to the port, and thence to the lane from which he had watched von Stalhein and Brandt emerge from Gestapo head-quarters.

'This will do,' he said. 'Stop here. It's unlikely that anyone will touch the car. Let's walk.'

They got out of the car, closing the doors, and stood for a moment while they made a quick reconnaissance. Everything seemed quiet. There were a few soldiers about, and two storm-troopers were as usual on duty outside the Hotel Port. Biggles pointed out the building to Algy and told him what it was.

'Never mind about that—where are these planes you

spoke about?' demanded Algy impatiently. 'I'm getting nervous.'

Biggles's eyes explored the harbour, but not a single machine could he see.

'They've gone,' he said simply.

'What!'

'I'm afraid it's true. The last time I was here there were at least a dozen machines on the water. If it comes to that, there were also far more vessels here then than there are now. Where the dickens have they all gone? Something must have happened. Just a minute—you wait here. I'm going to find out what's going on.'

'How?'

'By walking across to those troops and asking them—or listening to their conversation. I'll also have a good look at the harbour and make sure that there isn't a machine available.' Biggles walked away.

He was gone about ten minutes.

'Here, don't leave me like that again,' protested Algy when he returned. 'I can't speak German like you can, and if I'd been questioned by anybody I should have been sunk. Well, did you find out anything?'

'Yes. It seems that we've landed an expeditionary force—in fact, two or three as far as I can make out. The nearest is just south of Bergen. Another landing has been made at Trondheim.'

'How does that help us?'

'It doesn't, unless we can get to one of those places. But it's worth knowing.'

'Did you find a machine, that's what I want to know?'

'No.'

'So what? We can't stay here. We've got to get some

place, and before daylight, too. I'm nearly asleep on my feet, anyway.'

Biggles thought for a moment. 'The question is, dare we use the car?'

'It's risky.'

'There's no doubt about that, but we shan't get far on foot—even when we've decided where to go.'

'How far away is Bergen?'

'The best part of a hundred and fifty miles, but I gather that the landing has been made somewhere south of the actual town, so the distance may not be more than a hundred and twenty or a hundred and thirty miles.'

'That's a long way. How far is it to Ginger—to Fiord 21?'

'About thirty miles farther on to the north. Our nearest point of contact with our people is Bergen. We might try getting through that way. If we can't, we'll go on to Fiord 21. We shall have to go on there sooner or later, anyway, to make contact with Ginger and let him know that we've got clear of Boda; but since Bergen is nearer, we might borrow an aircraft or get someone to run up to the fiord with a message for Ginger.'

'Yes, that sounds the best plan,' agreed Algy.

Biggles nudged him. 'Just a minute. Don't speak while this fellow is going by.'

The man to whom Biggles had referred was in civilian clothes, and Algy assumed, not unnaturally, that he was a Norwegian. With bent head, as if deep in thought, he was walking quickly along the pavement. Not until he drew level with the car did he raise his head and look Biggles in the face.

Recognition was mutual and instantaneous. It was Brandt, the existence of whom Biggles had almost forgotten. He was, no doubt, on his way to his headquarters at the Hotel Port.

The German opened his mouth to shout, but the only sound that passed his lips was a grunt. Biggles's left fist shot out and took him in the pit of the stomach; then, as his head jerked forward, Biggles right flashed up in a vicious hook to the jaw. Brandt went over backwards; his head came into violent contact with the wall at the back of the pavement, and he lay still. The whole incident occurred in two seconds.

Biggles looked swiftly up and down the lane, then at Algy. 'This fellow knows me,' he said by way of explanation, for Algy, who had, of course, been unaware of this, had stared at the proceedings with amazement. 'We daren't leave him here,' went on Biggles tersely. 'Help me to get him in the back of the car.'

Not without difficulty, for Brandt was a heavy man, they bundled the limp body into the rear seat, from where it slid in a heap to the floor.

'You get in the back and take care of him,' ordered Biggles. 'I'll drive. I know my way about better than you do.'

As he spoke Biggles got swiftly into the driving seat. Algy jumped in behind. The doors slammed. The car shot out into the road and cruised up the main street.

'Where are you going?' asked Algy.

'We'll stick to our plan and make for Bergen. If we can't make contact with the British force there we'll push on to Fiord 21. I'd go right on to the fiord if I was certain we could get there, but now these landings have been made there's no knowing what we shall run into.'

'What are we going to do with this fellow? Are you going to take him with us all the way?'

'Not on your life. We'll dump him at some lonely place from which it will take him a long time to get into touch with Oslo.'

Biggles drove on into the night, heading north. For twenty miles he travelled at a cruising speed, careful not to attract attention to himself by fast driving; then, reaching a wild stretch of country, he stopped.

'We'll leave Brandt here,' he said quietly.

The German was now semi-conscious. That is to say his eyes were open, but he seemed dazed—as doubtless he was, for the blow he had received on the head was a severe one.

'Gestapo policy would be to bump him off, and so remove all risk of his setting the country on to us,' murmured Algy reflectively.

'Probably you're right, but Gestapo policy isn't ours,' returned Biggles briefly. 'Let's get on.'

Leaving Brandt half sitting, half reclining, against a rock where he would be seen by the first passer-by when daylight came, they re-entered the car and continued their journey.

'We must be getting pretty close to Bergen,' remarked Algy after a long interval of silence.

'It can't be more than ten miles,' replied Biggles.

'If our fellows landed there, then there must be Germans here too,' said Algy thoughtfully. 'Hasn't it struck you as odd that there's no sound of a battle?'

'Yes, there's something funny about that,' agreed

Biggles. 'However, we're likely to run into troops at any moment. If we do I'll ask them what's happening.'

Before long they reached the German forces. There was no need to seek them. The car was stopped by a patrol.

Biggles got out, his pass in his hand. 'It's all right,' he said casually. 'We've got orders to keep watch for suspicious characters. What's happening here?'

The German he addressed, a sergeant, did not question his presence there, or his authority. 'It's all over,' he startled Biggles by stating.

'All over—what do you mean?'

'The British have gone.'

'Gone?' Biggles was flabbergasted.

'Yes—we kicked them back into the sea.'

Biggles laughed, but there was little humour in his voice. 'Good work,' he said. 'Well, we'll get on. By the way, we're patrolling the coast northward; will there be any difficulty about getting through?'

'If you keep straight on there may be,' replied the sergeant. 'There are barricades across the road and troops are moving. But if you take the next turning to the right it will take you right out of the battle zone.'

'And if I turn left again farther on will that bring me back to the coast?' Biggles had taken out his map and was looking at it in the light of a headlamp.

'Yes, you could do that,' agreed the sergeant.

'Then we'll try it,' declared Biggles, folding the map and putting it back into his pocket. He got into the car and drove on.

'Phew! That was a bit of a bone-shaker,' said Algy in a strained voice. 'I wonder what made our fellows withdraw?'

'It's no use guessing,' returned Biggles briefly. 'We've got to get to Fiord 21 now, or we shall be in a mess. We've got to get there before daylight, too. There is this about it, we're not likely to run into any opposition so far north. You try to get a spot of sleep. Later on you can relieve me at the wheel and I'll have a map. The worst of these jobs is, one doesn't get time to eat or sleep.'

'Good thing we've had a bit of practice at it,' observed Algy, smiling weakly. He snuggled back, in his seat and closed his eyes.

Biggles drove on. He was tired to the point of exhaustion, and it was only by keeping a fierce hold on himself that he prevented himself from falling asleep over the wheel. He seemed to have been driving for an eternity. At last, as the grey of dawn stained the eastern sky, realizing that his endurance was at an end, he stopped the car and nudged Algy, who awoke with a start.

'Take the wheel,' said Biggles. 'I'm about played out.'

They exchanged seats, and Biggles sank back with a weary sigh.

It seemed that he had no sooner closed his eyes than he was being violently shaken.

'Brace yourself,' said Algy tersely. 'We're there—or as near as we can get to the fiord by staying on the road. What had I better do with the car?'

'Anything you like—we shan't need it again,' muttered Biggles. 'Perhaps you'd better drive into that gully just ahead. Nobody's likely to see it there, and it won't give rise to inquiries should the Germans come along.'

Algy obediently drove the car off the road into a

narrow gorge, the sides of which were thick with stunted firs. They got out at once, closed the doors and returned to the road. By the time they reached it pink dawn had lighted the wild landscape, enabling them to see for a considerable distance, but to their relief no one was in sight. Some distance to the left lay the sea; nearer, a jagged ridge marked the crest of the cliff that hemmed in the fiord.

'Thank goodness,' ejaculated Biggles. 'If Ginger hasn't got into trouble we're as good as home.'

Walking briskly, they soon reached the ridge. Throwing themselves flat, for it was a nasty drop into the fiord, they looked down. Neither spoke, although Algy hissed through his teeth.

Ginger's machine was not there. But the fiord was not abandoned. On its placid surface floated a squadron of Dornier flying-boats.

# Chapter 11
# Complications

Biggles was the first to break the silence. He lay still, staring down into the fiord.

'It looks as if I was not the only one who realized that this fiord would make a useful operating base,' he said bitterly.

'You're dead right there,' agreed Algy, gazing down into the fiord, which presented a scene of lively animation. In addition to the flying-boats there were two store-ships, from which were being unloaded war materials of many descriptions. A large green and brown camouflaged tent had already been erected on the one spot available, and into this the stores were being carried by several men. A little group of pilots sat on the rocks near the machines, smoking.

'What do you suppose became of Ginger?' asked Algy, after he had gazed at the scene for a few minutes.

'We can only guess,' returned Biggles slowly. 'If he was here when this crowd arrived they might have sunk him before he could get off the water. Not necessarily, of course. He would certainly hear them coming, and by acting quickly might have got clear. On the other hand, if he came back and found this lot here, obviously he wouldn't land. From the fact that I can't see any trace of his machine, or any quantity of oil on the water, I'm inclined to think he got away. In that case, knowing that we intended coming here, he'd stick around. There need be no doubt about that.'

'Then where is he now?'

'He might be sitting in another fiord not far away, or he might have gone off to get a load of bombs to knock the daylight out of these Dorniers.'

'The question is, what are we going to do about it?'

Biggles smiled faintly. 'Laddie, there are times when you ask the most difficult questions. I'm dashed if I know what to do for the best, and that's a fact. Personally, I should like to curl up and have a nice long sleep, but this doesn't seem to be either the time or the place for a nap. We're not out here on a pleasure cruise; we're here primarily to gather information about the enemy. If, incidentally, we can make life hard for him, then it's up to us to do it. We ought to let our people know that these Dorniers are sitting here. They've got some scheme on, no doubt. By watching them we may learn what it is. In any case, we daren't go away, because if we do we shall certainly lose touch with Ginger. Sooner or later he'll come back, and our only chance of making contact with him is to remain here. Give me a minute to think.'

Biggles was still squatting among the rocks that lined the rim of the fiord, concentrating hard, when from out of the west came the roar of aero engines.

'There they are,' hissed Algy, pointing to a line of tiny black specks that had emerged from the thin mist that hung over the sea. 'They look as if they're coming straight to this spot.'

By this time Biggles was on his knees, stiff with excitement. 'You're right,' he rapped out. 'They're our

boys, too, if I know the sweet song of Merlin engines.*
By gosh I've got it. Ginger has fetched them to bomb
the place. Keep your head down. This is going to be a
warm spot in a minute.'

As they drew near, the machines, which it was now
possible to identify as Skuas** of the Fleet Air Arm,
dived steeply. The Germans, of course, had seen them
coming, and everything below was in a state of something like panic. Some of the pilots were getting into
their machines. Mechanics ran for cover, or hastily
mounted machine-guns. Engines burst into life. Smoke
poured from the funnels of the store-ships, but, gener-
ally speaking, the Germans had no time to establish an
adequate defence.

Lying on the rocks Biggles and Algy watched the raid
with bated breath. In line ahead, the British machines,
flying low, swept up the fiord, and as they passed over
the German camp a cloud of bombs went down. Spouts
of water leapt high into the air, while echoes flung back
the thunder of the explosions. After the first salvo the
watchers could see nothing, for the fiord was filled with
smoke, above which circled the Skuas, dropping the
remainder of their bombs, or, when these were exhaus-
ted, firing into the rising cloud of smoke with their
machine-guns.

Biggles, watching the machines, had no difficulty in
picking out Ginger's seaplane, for it kept a little apart
from the rest.

'There he is,' he told Algy. 'We've got to attract his
attention. He'll be on the watch for us.'

* British Rolls-Royce engines widely used in World War II fighter and
bomber aircraft.
** Royal Navy carrier-borne dive bombers.

He sprang to his feet, but before he could do anything in the way of making a signal the smoke, rising from the fiord as from the crater of a volcano, hid everything from view.

'Confound the smoke,' snarled Biggles. 'It's going to jigger us. For all we know Ginger may have already spotted us. If he has he'll land on the fiord—or at the entrance to it. I'll tell you what. You stay here in case the smoke clears, in which case he'd be more likely to see you up here than down below. I'll go down to the water to see if he has landed. If he has I'll dash back here and let you know.'

Biggles made for the landslide which, as far as he knew, was the only way down into the fiord. The smoke was still rising, so visibility improved as he went down, and by the time he reached the water level he could see for some distance. He noted that one of the store-ships was in flames; the other appeared to have run aground. At least five of the Dorniers had been wrecked; two had been beached, and the remaining two were taxi-ing at high speed towards the open sea. But he was not concerned with these things at the moment, for Ginger was just landing. As soon as it was on the water the seaplane swung round and roared towards the place where Biggles stood.

Ginger, white with excitement, stood up in the cock-pit and yelled, 'Where's Algy?'

'He waiting on top!' shouted Biggles. 'We weren't sure if you'd spotted us. Stand fast—I'll fetch him.'

Without wasting words, Biggles set off back up the landslide, little guessing what he was to find at the top.

Algy had followed his instructions to the letter; that is, he had remained on the edge of the cliff overlooking the fiord. And, lying there, he distinctly heard Ginger hail Biggles—and, in fact, heard the brief conversation that passed between them. Yet, knowing the danger of departing from a fixed plan, he dared not leave the spot, for the smoke was thick around him, and there was a risk that if he started down the landslide he might pass Biggles without seeing him. If that happened then Biggles would arrive at the top only to wonder what had become of him. What he did was to fling his German greatcoat aside, for it impeded his movements more than a little; at the same time he stood up ready to make a dash towards Biggles the moment he saw him. He heard someone coming, and he thought, not unnaturally, that it was Biggles, although it struck him that there was a lot of noise being made by one person. Then, before he could move, out of the smoke burst a crowd of Germans—a few officers and the rest mechanics. One of the officers was still carrying a sub-machine-gun, with which, presumably, he had been firing at the raiders. The instant he saw Algy he covered him.

The whole thing was so unexpected, and had happened so suddenly, that Algy had no time to do anything. Indeed, at that moment he wouldn't have given a fig for his life, for the Germans were wild with excitement, and seemed likely to fire at him anyway. At point blank range they could hardly miss. In the circumstances, self-preservation came first, and Algy probably did the wisest thing he could do. He put his hands up.

Panting, the Germans closed in around him.

'So we got one of you,' said the officer who carried the machine-gun, in fair English.

Algy nodded ruefully. His brain was still in a whirl.

The officer smiled. He appeared to bear Algy no particular animosity. 'Hot work, eh?' he said, as one pilot to another.

'Very hot,' agreed Algy bitterly, wondering what was going to happen next.

At that moment Biggles appeared over the rim of the fiord, not ten yards away. He stopped dead when he saw the crowd, but then came on again. He saw at a glance what had happened—that somehow Algy had got mixed up with fugitives from the raid.

'Hullo, what's all this?' he asked.

'We got one of them,' answered the officer who had spoken to Algy. Then a puzzled expression leapt to his face. 'Where have you come from?' he inquired. 'You weren't one of us.'

As we know, Biggles was in German uniform, but as the officer had remarked, he was not one of the squadron that had been raided. Obviously it was no use trying to pretend that he was.

'I was just flying into the fiord when the British arrived,' he announced calmly. 'There wasn't room to turn. Then the bombs burst and in the smoke I couldn't see a thing. I managed to get down, only to crash against the rocks and sink my machine. After that I did what you evidently did—saw about getting out of the way until the British had gone.'

The German officer laughed. He seemed to be a cheerful sort of fellow. It was obvious that no suspicion of the true state of affairs had entered his mind. Indeed, there was no reason why it should.

'Well, here we are,' he said. 'The British didn't waste any time in finding us and smoking us out.'

Biggles got off this dangerous subject. 'What are you going to do with this prisoner?' he asked—speaking, of course, in German.

'We shall have to take him with us. We can't do anything else.'

'And where are you going—I'm a stranger in these parts myself.'

'So am I,' confessed the officer readily. 'It looks as if we shall have to walk, and try to find a telephone to get into touch with head-quarters. I'm afraid there will be trouble about this. We'd got an important assignment.'

'In that case I'll come with you,' said Biggles wearily.

Meanwhile, Ginger, standing in his cockpit down on the fiord, could not understand why Biggles and Algy did not come. Naturally, he expected them down immediately, but when the minutes passed and they still had not come, he realized that something had gone wrong; but what it was he could not imagine. Presently, as the smoke began to clear, a rifle cracked and the bullet zipped through his fuselage. A moment later another whistled unpleasantly close to his head, and looking across the water he saw that the sailors on the store-ship which had run aground were shooting at him. Obviously he could not remain where he was, for he would soon be under the fire of every German who had survived the raid. All he could do was open the throttle and take off, hoping that from the air he would be able to locate the others and somehow pick them up.

He soon saw them; he also saw the Germans and guessed pretty well what had happened. There was nothing he could do, and when the Germans opened fire on him with rifles and a machine-gun he lost no time in removing himself from such a dangerous position. The other British machines had already disappeared out to sea. For a little while, from a distance, he watched the party walking inland along the edge of the cliff. Then, feeling utterly helpless, he turned away and headed north.

Biggles and Algy watched him go—without comment, of course, for their attitude towards each other was that of captor and captured. Algy strode along with a mechanic on either side of him. Biggles stayed with the officers. Some were glum; others were cheerful, and, where Algy was concerned, inclined to be sympathetic. They were well able to appreciate his position.

They came to a farmhouse where they stopped, drank milk, and made a frugal meal. The Norwegian to whom it belonged was in no case to refuse what was asked of him. After a short rest they went on to the main road—the same road over which Biggles had passed earlier in the day. And while they were standing on it, undecided which way to go, a motor-cyclist storm-trooper came tearing along. He stopped and dismounted when he saw the party, and was soon told what had happened.

'I shall have to let head-quarters know about this,' he declared. 'I'm on the trail of two British spies, and they may have had something to do with the raid. You'd better keep your eyes open for them.'

He actually made this request to Biggles, who promised that if the spies fell into his hands they would have short shrift.

As the motor-cyclist went on Biggles wondered why he had addressed him, and saw for the first time that he was the senior officer of the party, in that he was an Oberleutnant—or wore the uniform of one—whereas the others were only Leutnants. He determined forthwith to take advantage of this, and from that moment more or less placed himself in command of the party.

'I'm by no means sure that we did right in leaving the fiord,' he told the other officers. 'I don't know about you, but I'm by no means clear as to what has happened there. Head-quarters may send new machines up, so I'm wondering if, instead of wandering about the country like this, out of touch with everybody, it wouldn't be better for us to go back there.'

What Biggles really wanted was time to think, to form a definite plan. At present he had none, and the appearance of the motor-cyclist made it only too clear that they could not continue for long to move about the country without being arrested. Moreover, the farther they got from the fiord, the farther they were getting away from Ginger, their only contact with home, and their only means of escape. He noted that from time to time squadrons of German planes passed high overhead, all heading northward, and he asked the Germans if they knew the meaning of this.

The senior Leutnant smiled knowingly. 'Haven't you heard?' he said softly.

His manner was so mysterious that Biggles was intrigued. At the same time he was conscious of a disturbing uneasiness.

'No, I haven't heard anything,' he said.

'Then you were not on the same job as us, that's certain.' The Leutnant hesitated, but then went on, confidentially. 'Keep this to yourself,' he whispered, 'but the British North Sea Fleet is sailing into a lovely trap.'

Biggles did not move a muscle. 'How?' he asked.

'Well, to start with, they are going to land troops at Narvik—our Intelligence people know that for a fact. To cover the landing the British fleet will use, as a base, Westfiord, which is handy. Our spies watched them survey the place for that purpose, and they're heading straight for it now. But what they don't know is this. Since they were there we have been busy. We've stuffed the fiord with magnetic mines* until it is as full of them as a pudding is of plums. When the ships sail in there'll be one big bang, and that will be the end of them. Meanwhile, the British troops won't know this. They'll attempt to land at Narvik and then our planes will shoot them to bits. Our machines are concentrating up there now for that purpose.'

Biggles felt a cold hand settle over his heart. He moistened his lips. 'You're quite certain about this fiord, Westfiord, being full of mines?'

'I ought to be,' grinned the German. 'My squadron put them there. That's what we've been doing.'

Biggles smiled—but only with his lips. There was no humour in his eyes, for this staggering piece of news and its deadly significance altered all his ideas. The trap sounded such a likely one that he did not doubt the authenticity of it for a moment.

Algy was standing close enough to hear what had been said, but his expression did not change. His eyes met those of Biggles only for a moment, but they held a question.

* Underwater mines detonated when the hull of a passing vessel causes a shift of the magnetic field at the mine.

As far as they were concerned, from that moment escape became of secondary importance. The only thing that mattered was getting a warning to the ships of the Royal Navy engaged in the enterprise, and to the commander of the troops bound for Narvik.

Said Biggles to the Leutnant: 'I believe two of your machines escaped when the raid started. D'you think they'll come back?'

'They're almost certain to, if only to see what has happened,' returned the German without hesitation.

'In that case,' observed Biggles quietly, 'I think we'd better get back there. The machines would at least enable us to get into touch with headquarters.'

'I think you're right there,' agreed the other. 'What about the prisoner?'

Biggles shrugged his shoulders, as if the matter was a minor one. 'It looks as if we shall have to keep him with us—for the time being, at any rate.'

'He may get in the way,' demurred the Leutnant. 'Remember, he's a pilot, so it won't do to let him get near an aircraft.'

Biggles nodded. The last thing he wanted was to be parted from Algy. 'Trondheim is the nearest depot,' he pointed out. 'And that's nearly forty miles away,' he added. 'The only thing we can do with the prisoner for the moment is to keep him with us. If a machine comes into the fiord we may be able to get rid of him then, either by flying him up to Trondheim, or by sending him to Oslo.'

'Yes, that seems to be the best plan,' agreed the Leutnant.

They set off back towards the fiord.

# Chapter 12
# Desperate Measures

It was past midday when they got back to the fiord, to find that it had more or less settled down. There was a fair amount of wreckage floating on the water. One of the store-ships had burnt itself out; the other was still aground, in spite of the efforts of the survivors of both crews to get her off. A little party of airmen, apparently odd members of the squadron that had dispersed when the raid occurred, were sitting or standing about the spot where the store-tent had stood. Biggles noted that, as so often happens, the sailors and the airmen, members of two services, kept apart from each other, as if they were acting under separate orders—as no doubt they were. Those airmen who had remained at the fiord greeted the return of the others with cheers.

From the top of the landslide, which was the easiest way down to the water, Biggles surveyed the fiord. 'No aircraft have arrived yet,' he observed.

The Leutnant declared that it could only be a matter of time before something, or somebody, arrived, for news of the raid must by then have reached either Trondheim or Oslo, perhaps both. It was a reasonable assumption, and the party made its way to the others on the rocky beach, where the raid was discussed. Algy, under guard, sat a little apart from the others. Biggles, of course, mixed freely with the Germans.

This state of affairs lasted for about an hour, during which time Biggles racked his brains in vain to find a way out of the curious position in which he and Algy now found themselves. Things might, he thought, have been worse. At least he had his liberty, and had it not been for the disquieting information about the trap which had been prepared for the British fleet he would have been content to wait quietly until something turned up. He still felt that his best chance of getting away lay in remaining at the fiord, because Ginger knew that they must be there, or in the vicinity. So there seemed no point in leaving. Even if he, Biggles, and Algy could get clear, they would only wander about the country without a definite objective. True, there was the car which they had concealed, but he felt that by this time it would be a dangerous vehicle to take on the road. Whether or not word had gone out for that particular car to be apprehended, it would certainly be stopped by every patrol, and with so few roads it would be impossible to get far without encountering patrols. Indeed, Biggles had a shrewd suspicion that a proper hue and cry had been started for them. Brandt, whom they had left by the roadside, and who by now must have been picked up, would probably see to that.

It was, then, with relief that after they had been back in the fiord about an hour Biggles saw a flying-boat approaching. It was a Dornier, and was recognized immediately by the members of the squadron for one of their own. Biggles caught Algy's eye and winked, for this was what he had been waiting for. He resolved that this was the machine that should carry them to safety. There was no other way.

The Dornier landed and taxied up to the beach,

where it was made fast by one of the airmen who had walked forward to meet it. The pilot came ashore to be greeted with a volley of questions.

'Where have you been?' asked one of the German officers.

'I dashed down to Oslo to report the raid,' was the reply. 'They sent me back with orders that we are to stand fast here until help is sent. I suppose they will send us new machines.'

Biggles was staring at the pilot in alternate alarm and satisfaction, for it was none other than Schaffer, the officer whom he had first met at Narvik, and who had afterwards flown him to Boda; in fact, it was Schaffer's uniform that he was still wearing. And at that moment, looking round, Schaffer saw him. An extraordinary expression at once crossed his face.

'Hello, what are you doing here?' he said moving forward slowly at the same time.

Biggles forced a smile. 'I deserve all you must have thought of me for not returning your uniform,' he said in tones of self-reproach. 'As you see, I'm still wearing it, but to tell the truth I've been so rushed since I last saw you that I haven't had time to see about getting it back to you.'

Schaffer still gazed at Biggles with a peculiar expression on his face. A struggle seemed to be going on inside him.

As for Biggles, he could well imagine what Schaffer was thinking. It is a far cry from being merely suspicious to making a direct accusation; but that Schaffer was suspicious was obvious; or, if not actually suspicious, he felt that there was something odd going on. What Biggles did not know, and perhaps it was as well for his peace of mind that he did not, was the extent of the hue and cry that had been started for him. He did not know that every German agent and every patrol in Norway was looking for him; and this being so, strange rumours were afoot, rumours that had reached the ears of nearly every German in the country, including Schaffer. Unaware of this, although he dimly suspected something of the sort, Biggles did not take it into account. He saw Schaffer hesitating, and had a good idea of what was in his mind. He knew that the German was wondering if he ought to cross-examine him there and then, and perhaps accuse of being a spy, or wait until he could get through to Oslo and leave this task to those whose specific duty it was to attend to such things.

What Schaffer actually did was to walk a short distance away taking the other officers with him. These he engaged in earnest conversation, and from covert glances thrown in his direction Biggles knew that he was the object of the discussion. It was quite apparent that even if nothing worse happened, from that moment he was a marked man, and the first false move he made would be quite enough to fan smouldering suspicion into the flame of direct action. He glanced at the machine riding on the water, and then at Algy, wondering if he ought to risk all on a sudden dash for liberty. It was one of those difficult decisions upon which so much might depend. At the finish he decided against the plan, chiefly because there were so many Germans about that to hope for success was to hope for something in the nature of a miracle.

He made a swift survey of the weaknesses in his position, for they were plain enough to see. When Schaffer compared notes with the others—and that was undoubtedly what he was doing at that moment—they would perceive that there was something very odd in the manner in which he had appeared, from nowhere, so to speak. And the same with Algy. Up to now it had been assumed automatically that he was one of the British raiding party, and had been shot down. But what had happened to his machine? No one had seen it fall. There was no crash to mark the spot. Biggles felt that once the Germans started thinking on these lines, and they could hardly fail to do so, his freedom would not last long.

He was not told what the result of the conference was. He was able to form an idea of it, however, when, a few minutes later, he noticed that two of the airmen, armed with rifles, were never far away from him. And when a little while later Schaffer came over and told him, with a nonchalance that was obviously affected, that he was flying to Oslo, and invited him to go with him, Biggles understood the general scheme. Schaffer was not prepared to run the risk of arresting one who might in fact turn out to be a member of the dreaded Gestapo; instead, he would get him to Oslo and put the onus of responsibility for this on someone else.

Biggles answered at once that he would be glad to go. He could not very well do otherwise. Nor dared he hesitate, knowing how thin was the hair on which his freedom depended.

'In that case we'll take off right away,' said Schaffer.

As these words were spoken Biggles saw Algy being taken along the beach towards the supply-ship, which, for want of something better adapted to the purpose, was evidently to be his temporary prison. It was not a very desirable one, for from remarks let drop by the airmen Biggles knew that it was loaded with petrol and ammunition. Indeed, he could see some of the oil drums which had been put ashore to lighten the ship, evidently in the hope that it would float off the rock on which it was aground at the next high tide.

Biggles told Schaffer that he had no kit to collect, so he was ready to move off. He still had a card up his sleeve, and it was this. Schaffer did not know that he was a pilot. The fact that he wore a pilot's uniform meant nothing—at least, as far as the German was concerned, for he knew that it was his own. Biggles hoped, therefore that he would be able to overpower Schaffer in the air and seize the machine. His chief fear was that other officers might be in it—more than he could deal with.

Great was his relief when, a minute or two later, Schaffer beckoned to him and led the way towards the aircraft, for it was clear that the others were remaining in the fiord.

'Where would you like to sit?' inquired Schaffer.

Not for a moment did Biggles abandon his original pose of quiet assurance. 'Well, I'm a bit nervous of these things, you know,' he said, simulating slight embarrassment. 'If it's all the same to you I'd like to sit beside you.' He had noted that there was side-by-side seating in the Dornier, but only one set of controls.

Schaffer agreed so readily that Biggles became more and more convinced that the last thing the German expected was that he might be attacked in the air. Indeed, if, as he supposed, Biggles was a mere land-lubber, then he had nothing to fear on that score, for no one but a lunatic—or, of course, another pilot— would interfere with a man at the controls of an aircraft.

They took their places. The machine was cast off, and Schaffer taxied out to the middle of the fiord to take off.

'There's a chance that we may run into hostile aircraft,' he announced. 'If we do just sit tight and leave things to me.'

'You bet I will,' promised Biggles. 'I'm afraid I shouldn't be much use.'

Schaffer opened the throttle. The flying-boat sped across the water and rose like a bird into the air. For a little while the pilot held the machine straight, climbing steeply for altitude, and then banked round in the direction of his destination.

Biggles knew that it was not much more than half an hour's flight, so he had no time to lose. No sooner were they out of sight of the fiord than he opened the proceedings by very gently taking Schaffer's revolver from its holster. He had a pistol of his own in his pocket, but he felt that if he disarmed the German as a first precaution it would make his task easier.

He was in the act of putting the revolver into his own pocket when Schaffer happened to glance round. He saw at once what was happening. Fear and anger leapt into his eyes.

'What are you—' he began, but Biggles cut him short.

'I'm sorry, Schaffer,' he said curtly. 'I must ask you to let me have this machine. I should be sorry to have to hurt you, so I hope you'll be reasonable about it.'

Schaffer had turned as white as a sheet. His eyes blazed.

'Then I was right,' he hissed. 'You are a spy.'

'It would be futile to deny it,' admitted Biggles, 'but if I am it is by force of circumstances and not as a result of any desire on my part. Actually, like you, I am a pilot. I was caught in Oslo when the war started and I've been trying to get home ever since. I am now going. Please vacate your seat.'

'I will not,' snarled Schaffer, and abandoning the controls, he flung himself at Biggles in such a fury that Biggles was taken by surprise. Before he could prevent it Schaffer's left hand had caught him by the throat, forcing him back into his seat.

Biggles deliberately kicked the joystick, and then, hooking his leg round it, dragged it back. The machine plunged, and then reared up like a frightened horse. Instinctively the German spun round to right the aircraft, which was in danger of falling into a spin, but Biggles now caught him by the arms, and thrusting his knee in the small of his back, flung him back into the cabin. He then made a dive for the controls to prevent the machine from stalling.

Schaffer went at him again. He appeared to have gone mad.

'Look out, you fool!' yelled Biggles. 'You'll kill us both.'

Schaffer's only reply was to hook an arm round his neck.

Now if there is one thing a man cannot do it is fly an aeroplane and fight at the same time. The controls of a modern high-performance aircraft are extremely sensitive, and a movement of an inch of the joystick or rudder is sufficient to throw a machine out of level flight. To any violent movement of the controls an aircraft responds instantly.

In his efforts to free himself Biggles was compelled to release the controls, with the result that the machine was left to its own devices. His aim now was to break clear from the clinch in which Schaffer held him in order to get his hand into his pocket for his pistol. Schaffer knew this, and hung on like grim death. Locked in fierce embrace, they surged up and down the cabin. Still locked, they fell, and rolled towards the tail. Their weight caused the nose to rise, with the result that the machine stalled, and then plunged earthward like a stone. Torn apart by the rush through space, both antagonists were flung against the instrument board. Through the windscreen Biggles saw the rock-bound coast leaping towards them, and realized that if something were not done instantly to check the fall, they were both doomed.

'Wait!' he yelled, and gabbing the joystick, eased the machine out to level flight. It finished only a few hundred feet above the cliffs.

Schaffer, panting with rage and exertion, fingers hooked ready to resume the struggle, waited.

But Biggles had had enough of this sort of fighting. One more bout like the last, now that they had no height to spare, would be the end. Satisfied that the machine was trimmed to fly straight, he whipped out the revolver—which Schaffer appeared to have forgotten—and covered the German.

'One move and I shall have to shoot,' he threatened. 'Believe me, I don't want to have to do that, Schaffer, but if it is to be one or the other of us, it isn't going to be me.'

Schaffer made no answer, so Biggles, still watching him, got more securely into the pilot's seat. He flew with one hand on the control column. The other held the revolver.

'I'm going to land,' he said, snatching a glance at the sea, which looked calm enough for that operation. 'We'll finish the argument in more stable conditions.'

He cut the throttle and began gliding towards the water. After the roar of the engine the silence was uncanny. A more fantastic tableau it would be hard to imagine, and Schaffer evidently realized it, for a peculiar smile crept over his face.

'You English bring your nerve with you,' he conceded.

'No use leaving it at home,' returned Biggles lightly.

Another silence fell, broken only by the whine of wind over the wings.

The flying-boat was still a hundred feet above the water when into the silence burst the vicious clatter of machine-guns. A stream of bullets struck the hull. Glass flew from the instrument board, and splinters of three-ply from the fuselage.

Biggles steepened his dive. It was all he could do, for to examine the sky to locate the attacker would be to invite fresh trouble from Schaffer.

The German, however, was not prepared to submit so tamely. With a mutter of fury he flung open a small chest, of the purpose of which Biggles had been unaware, and dragged out a machine-gun.

Biggles acted with the speed of light. He jerked the throttle open and flung the machine into a vertical bank. Schaffer went over backwards, the gun crashing out of his hands. Biggles left the controls, snatched it up, and then jumped back into his seat. He was only just in time, for the machine, now within fifty feet of the water, was wobbling on the verge of another stall.

Schaffer, who seemed to be slightly dazed by his fall, staggered to his feet as the keel kissed the water. It was a bad landing, not surprising in the circumstances, but Biggles didn't mind. He was only concerned with getting the machine down. The flying-boat surged on to a standstill, while from outside came the roar of an aero-engine.

Looking through a side window, Biggles saw that he had come to rest within fifty yards of the shore, which at that point took the form of a cliff, fringed at the foot by a strip of sand. Opening the throttle a little, he urged the machine nearer to it.

'Can you swim?' he asked Schaffer grimly.

'Yes.'

'Then get going—it isn't far.'

Schaffer hesitated, but another burst of fire, which struck the machine aft, seemed to decide him.

'I shall be interested to watch the outcome of the argument between you and your countryman,' he said bitingly. 'We shall meet again.'

'Perhaps,' smiled Biggles. 'If we do I hope it will be after the war. Look me up at the Aero Club, and I'll stand you a dinner in return for the use of your uniform.'

Schaffer nodded curtly and jumped into the water.

Seeing that it only came up to his armpits, Biggles flicked the throttle open and taxied away towards more open water. From time to time above the roar of his engine he could still hear the harsh tattoo of machine-guns. He was soon in a position to take off, but before doing so he looked out to ascertain the nature of the machine that was attacking him. He knew, of course, that it must be a British machine, and assumed that it was either a patrolling formation of the Fleet Air Arm, or a lone scout. Curiously enough, the truth never occurred to him.

He gasped when he saw the machine overhead, for he recognized it at once. It was Ginger's sea-plane.

# Chapter 13
# Fresh Plans

To say that Biggles was shaken would be to put it mildly, yet on second thoughts he perceived that the fact that Ginger was in the other machine made little or no difference to the situation. He could not hope to be recognized at the distance which separated the aircraft even if he showed himself, and Ginger would naturally take him for an enemy. His problem was how to get away, for he could not engage in a fight with a British plane.

With his heart in his mouth, he proceeded to take off, for while he was doing so he was at a big disadvantage. However, as soon as he was off the water he held the machine down and looked back to see what Ginger was doing. He was not surprised to see him swooping down on his tail. And that was not all Biggles saw. High up behind Ginger's machine was a line of black specks, specks that grew larger even as he watched them. There was no need to look twice to see what was happening; it was all too plain. Ginger, intent only on his quarry, had allowed himself to be surprised by a German patrol, and it was obvious from the way he was flying that he was still blissfully unaware of it.

Biggles groaned. He felt that the situation was beyond him. It had been bad enough before the other machines appeared, but now it was so complicated that he almost abandoned hope of finding a solution. It came to this. By some means or other he had to prevent himself from being shot down by Ginger; at the same time he had to warn Ginger of what was happening behind his tail. To achieve this difficult object the only thing he could do, he decided, was to place himself between the seaplane and the German formation; then in looking at him Ginger would—or should—see his danger. After that he would have to rely on his own resources.

Things did not pan out as he had planned, however. He could see that he would fail, even before the worst happened, for by the time he had zoomed high preparatory to getting behind the seaplane, the German machines had closed in and had launched their attack.

Ginger at once half rolled, a manœuvre which told Biggles that he had perceived his danger. The rest was more or less a foregone conclusion, for the newcomers were Messerschmitt 110's,* and there were eight of them. Ginger, abandoning the Dornier, now did his utmost to get away, but the seaplane was outclassed, as well as outnumbered.

Sick at heart, Biggles landed to watch the end of the affair, for there was nothing he could do. White-faced, he threw open the cockpit cover and stared up at the circling machines. It could hardly be called a combat. Time and time again the Messerschmitts darted in at their prey, their guns spurting flame, and the great wonder to Biggles was that Ginger could hang on for so long. But the end came at last. A Messerschmitt came down on the tail of the luckless seaplane. Ginger swung round and pulled up his nose to meet it, but the next instant black smoke was pouring from his engine.

* German twin engine fighter, often abbreviated to ME110.

155

The seaplane at once went into a steep side-slip towards the sea, but while it was still two thousand feet above it flames licked out through the smoke. Ginger appeared. For a moment he stood poised on the fuselage. Then he jumped clear.

For a thousand feet he dropped like a stone, slowly turning over and over as he fell. Then a white ribbon flashed above him. It grew longer, and then his fall was checked as the parachute blossomed out.

A great gasp of relief burst from Biggles' lips as he dropped back into his seat. He pushed the throttle open, and in a moment was taxi-ing at dangerous speed towards the area where he judged Ginger would fall. There was a splash of foam as Ginger struck the sea.

Biggles reached the spot within a minute, but all he could see was the parachute fabric spreading out like an enormous jellyfish on the surface of the water. It was the work of a moment to cut the throttle, reach over the side and seize the shrouds. He seemed to be hauling for an eternity before Ginger appeared, puffing and blowing like a grampus.

Biggles never forgot the expression on Ginger's face as he dragged him into the machine and relieved him of the parachute, allowing it to fall back into the sea. Ginger collapsed in a heap on the floor of the cockpit. He was too far gone to speak. He could only gasp and get rid of vast quantities of sea water.

For the moment Biggles let him lie there. He wanted to get rid of the Messerschmitts, which were still circling round like a pack of hungry wolves. It was not a difficult matter. He merely climbed up on his centre-section and waved his arms, a signal which he hoped would be construed by the Germans as thanks for saving him, and at the same time convey to them that their assistance was no longer needed. Apparently the Messerschmitt pilots read the signal that way, for they at once reformed in formation and sped away to the south. Happening to glance towards the shore, a bare half mile away, Biggles saw a solitary figure standing on the edge of the cliff that frowned down on the strip of beach. He knew it could only be Schaffer, who must have chosen this grand-stand to watch the end of the affair.

Biggles waved a friendly greeting.

Schaffer waved back, and disappeared over the brow of a hill.

'Who the deuce are you waving to—Algy?' panted Ginger, dragging himself into a sitting position and wringing the water out of his hair.

'No—a friend of mine,' replied Biggles. 'A German named Schaffer. Not a bad chap when you get to know him. This is his uniform I'm wearing; and, incidentally, this is his machine. He'll have a tale to tell when he gets home.'

'By thunder! He's not the only one!' declared Ginger weakly, but with heavy sarcasm. 'So it was you I was trying to shoot down,' he added.

'Yes. Of course, you would have to choose me.'

'I was in the right mood to shoot down anybody,' declared Ginger.

'Are you hurt?'

'No, but I'm wet, and I'm cold, to say nothing of being tired and hungry,' announced Ginger. 'What about going home? I'm fed up with this. For the love of Mike, what's going on here, anyway? Where's Algy?'

'The Germans have got him. He's a prisoner in a store ship in the fiord.'

'I thought I'd cleared that bunch out,' swore Ginger furiously.

'You didn't do so badly,' grinned Biggles. 'One of the ships ran aground. The Boche have gone back there now, but they've no aircraft—at least, they hadn't any when I left. This was the only one, so I borrowed it. Schaffer decided to take me down to Oslo to find out just who I was; at least, that was the intention, but on the way down we had a little dispute as to who should do the flying—and I won.'

'So what?' demanded Ginger.

'There are two things we've got to do, and there's no time to be lost.'

'Is that all?' sneered Ginger. 'The last time I saw you there was only one thing to do, which was to get Algy out of Boda. Now there are two things. At the rate we're going there will soon be three.'

'I shouldn't be surprised,' sighed Biggles.

'Well, what are these things we've got to do?' demanded Ginger.

'First, get a message to the Admiralty. Second, get Algy out of the clutches of the Nazis.'

'Okay, go ahead,' invited Ginger. 'I can't think any more.'

'I'm afraid you'll have to try,' returned Biggles seriously, and described the trap into which the British fleet was steaming.

'What d'you suggest?' queried Ginger.

'We've got to move fast,' Biggles told him. 'Schaffer is ashore, and while he's got some way to go I expect he'll make for the fiord. We shall have to part company again. You put me ashore somewhere near the fiord, and then go on and warn the fleet about the trap. I'll try to get hold of Algy.'

'How am I going to get near the fleet in this swastika-painted kite? They'll shoot me to bits as soon as I show up.'

'That's a little problem you'll have to work out for yourself,' declared Biggles. 'But I think your best plan would be to locate the fleet, and then land on the water somewhere ahead, with your prop stopped. They won't shoot at you if they think you're disabled, and they'll certainly pick you up. Tell the skipper about the trap and ask him to send word to the troop transports.'

'Good enough,' agreed Ginger. 'Where shall I put you ashore?'

'Fly along the coast for about twenty miles; then anywhere will do.'

'And what are you going to do? I mean, how shall I get in touch with you again?'

'I shall make for the fiord and try to make contact with Algy. You'll have to come back and pick us up. You should have no difficulty in getting hold of a machine—you might even go on using this one. If I get Algy away we shall stick to the coast. You'll have to try to spot us; there's no other way. We'll make a smoke signal if we can. Now get going, or it will be dark, and then you'll have a job to find our ships.'

The sun was in fact fast sinking towards the horizon as Ginger took off and headed north, keeping close to the coastline. After a flight of ten minutes he landed again, near the entrance to a tiny fiord, into which he taxied.

'This will do fine,' announced Biggles.

'Suppose someone sees you go ashore?' queried Ginger.

'It won't matter, since I'm landing from a German machine, and in a German uniform,' Biggles pointed out, as Ginger taxied to a natural wharf so that Biggles could land dry-shod.

Biggles clambered up on the rocks. 'So long.' he called. 'Don't forget that everything depends on you now.'

Ginger waved. 'I'll get through,' he promised, and turned towards the open sea.

Biggles watched him take off, and then, making his way to the top of the cliff, he turned towards Fiord 21.

Ginger headed north-west, scanning the ever widening area of sea that became visible as he climbed higher and higher. It may seem strange that it had not occurred to him that he might be unable to find the ships he sought, but then it must be remembered that he was aware of their objective, and assumed that they would be steaming straight towards it; moreover, prior to his making contact with Biggles, his ship had actually been operating with the fleet, so he knew where it was at that time.

It was not until he had been flying for nearly an hour, by which time sea and sky had merged in a mysterious twilight, that doubts began to assail him, doubts that sharpened quickly to alarm as his petrol gauge fell back and neither ship nor 'plane broke the loneliness that surrounded him. In something like a panic he climbed higher in ever increasing circles. He could still see the rim of the sun, a slip of glowing gold, but he knew that it was invisible to those at sea level where purple shadows, fast darkening to sullen indigo, were obliterating the gently heaving water. With sinking heart he flew on, nursing his engine until the inevitable happened. It backfired as the petrol supply dried up; then it stopped altogether, and he had no alternative but to drop his nose and begin a long glide towards the sea. When, finally, he was compelled to land, he was in the grip of a despair such as he had seldom known. It was aggravated by a sense of impotence. He felt that he had let Biggles down; that he had let everyone down. Too late he realized that the last thing the fleet would do was to sail directly towards its objective.

There was absolutely nothing he could do except climb on to the centre-section and stare dumbly into the leaden darkness that surrounded him. Except for a gentle slap of wavelets against the hull of his machine, silence reigned. Fortunately for him the sea was calm, but he had no guarantee that it would remain so, and he was well aware that should the wind freshen, bringing with it a heavy sea, then his frail craft, with no means of maintaining headway, would quickly break up. Not that he thought very much about this; he was far too concerned over the failure of his mission.

How long he sat there he had no idea; he lost all count of time; but he reckoned that it was approaching midnight when he heard a distant sound that set the blood coursing through his veins. The sound was faint, but there was no mistaking it; it was the dull methodical beat of a heavy engine, but whether it was made by a British ship or a German Ginger had no means of knowing. The sound grew louder as the minutes passed, implying that the vessel was approaching, but as it showed no lights he was as yet unable to see it. He was showing no lights, either; nor, for that matter, had he any to show; so he was well aware that unless the vessel passed within hailing distance he would not be seen. The question that now arose, and he felt that it was a vital one, was this. Should he hail, or should he not? If he did, and the vessel turned out to be British, then all would be well; on the other hand, if it proved to be a German, then the worst would have happened. He decided to take the risk for since there were more British craft than German on the North Sea, he felt that the odds were in his favour.

A squat, bulky ship took shape in the darkness, not more than a cable's length away. Evidently the lookout did not see him, for it ploughed straight on without altering course, chugging into the darkness of the night on its unknown mission. Drawing a deep breath, and cupping his hands round his mouth, he let out a hail.

It was answered immediately.

'Ahoy there! Who are you?' came a voice—in English.

Ginger fairly gasped with relief. 'Friend!' he yelled back. 'I'm in an aircraft, on the water. I've run out of fuel.'

'Stand by while we come about,' sang the unseen sailor.

A bell rang and the black hull slowed down, churning the water as it swung round in a wide curve. In a few minutes it was alongside, and Ginger could just see a knot of figures near the rail discussing him in low tones. He heard someone say, 'Blimey! Look out, it's a Jerry bus.' Whereupon he called out that the machine was, in fact, a German plane in which he had been trying to escape, but had landed on account of fuel shortage.

No doubt his voice did much to prove his assertion,

and he was soon taken aboard what turned out to be a British armed trawler, under the command of a naval officer. The aircraft having been taken in tow, Ginger was led to a cabin, where he explained his plight to two keen-faced officers, one of whom was the captain. To them, hardly pausing for breath, he poured out his story, laying particular emphasis on the trap that had been laid in West-fiord for the British fleet. He also described the base which the Germans had established in Fiord 21, and mentioned the store-ship that was still there.

When he had finished he was given some refreshment while the naval officers withdrew to confer. 'Whatever you do you must stop the fleet,' he told them desperately. 'I suppose you've got wireless?'

'We have, but we're sailing under orders,' replied the captain. 'What's more, we're only supposed to use our radio in case of dire emergency. It's dangerous. The enemy can pick a message up as well as our people, don't forget.'

'But you've got a code.'

'Yes, we have,' admitted the naval officer, who seemed to be rather worried.

And that is all Ginger was told. The officers departed and a steward brought into the cabin a square meal, which pleased Ginger not a little, for he felt that he could now safely leave things to the Navy. Somehow or other they would do what was required. What he himself was going to do he did not know. Engrossed in his meal, and thinking of the present rather than of the future, he had not even considered this aspect when he was flung across the cabin by a fearful explosion which took him completely unawares. Instantly all the lights went out.

As he picked himself up he heard shouts on the deck above, and other noises which convinced him in a vague sort of way—for he was too shaken for lucid thought—that the ship had blown up. His meal forgotten, he made his way—not without difficulty for the trawler had taken on a heavy list—to the deck. He realized that some sailors near him were lowering a boat, but the darkness was such that he could see nothing distinctly; nor could he make out what was happening. The trawler lurched again, and almost before he was aware of his danger water was swirling round his legs. A sailor hurried past him, shouting, 'Swim for it, boys!'

Ginger would have asked him what had happened, but before he could do so the man had disappeared into the darkness. He moved forward, only to fall over what turned out to be a pile of lifebelts. Not knowing the ship, he had no idea where he was. There was no confusion; occasionally he saw forms in the gloom, but beyond the fact that the trawler was sinking he could not get a grasp on the situation. All he could see fairly clearly were the upper works of the vessel; they were leaning over at an angle so acute that they made him feel giddy. The doomed vessel lurched again, causing a great hissing of steam, and he realized that if he were to avoid being sucked down in the vortex, the sailor's advice to 'swim for it' was not to be ignored. Sliding across the deck, he jumped blindly into the sea, and as soon as he came to the surface he started swimming as fast as he could to place as great a distance as possible between him and the vessel. He could still see nothing, but there were shouts in the darkness around him. They sounded strangely unreal.

Whether he swam into the submarine, or whether it rose up under him, he never knew. He was suddenly aware of a black bulk right beside him, and, instinctively, he tried to climb on to it; but his clawing fingers could get no grip on the smooth metal. After that the whole thing became a nightmare. He didn't know what was happening and he didn't much care. The fact was that exhaustion and shock had reduced him to a state of semi-consciousness. In a dreamy sort of way he was aware of hands clutching at his jacket, and dragging him up. What happened after that he did not know.

# Chapter 14
# Trapped!

After he had watched Ginger out of sight Biggles made his way cautiously to the fiord. It took him some time to reach it, and if he had entertained any doubts about its still being occupied they were dispelled even before he reached the rim. Judging from numerous voices, and a certain amount of hammering, it sounded as if salvage work was in progress.

From the edge of the cliff, which by this time he knew well, he looked down; but all was shrouded in darkness, and except for a cluster of lights near the stranded store-ship, whence came the noise of hammering, he could see nothing. It was towards this ship that Algy had been led, so he assumed—and hoped—that he would be in it. All his plans for rescue depended on that one fact. If Algy was not there, then he would not know where to look for him; but if he had been confined in the ship, then one factor was in his favour. He had not failed to note that the airmen and the sailors went about their work almost unmindful of each other, so there seemed a reasonable chance that, although the German airmen had been informed by Schaffer of his suspicions concerning Biggles's real identity, the sailors knew nothing about it. After all, he thought, as far as the officers of the air squadron were concerned, he, Biggles, was by this time safely lodged in Oslo; and there appeared to be no reason why they should discuss the matter with the sailors. If that were so, then the sailors would know nothing about him. They would not know him by sight even if they saw him, and they certainly would not be prepared for an attempt to rescue their prisoner.

Biggles made his way down the landslide without any great difficulty, but he took no chances and moved with extreme caution. Having reached the water-level, he then had to make his way along it to the rock on which the ship was beached. Fortunately it lay between him and the airmen's camp, so he was saved the difficult business of getting through that. Looking along the beach, he could just make out the silhouette of a Dornier flying-boat riding at anchor a few yards from the shore, and he noted its position carefully.

What concerned him now was the fact that the ship lay a short distance out—perhaps thirty or forty yards. In order that the sailors could get to and fro, an improvised gangway, consisting of a number of planks, had been erected. This gangway was in constant use, and on the face of it, it appeared to be out of the question to get on board without coming face to face with some of the sailors. Admittedly, he was wearing a German officer's uniform, so there was a chance that the seamen would take no notice of him. Even if he were questioned, he thought, he might be able to bluff his way through. Nevertheless, this involved a certain amount of risk which would be better avoided if it were possible. After considering the problem for a little while he decided he would only use the gangway if he could find no other means of getting on board.

Moving nearer, he was delighted but not altogether surprised to see on the water, close to the narrow strip of beach, a small collapsible canoe, of the sort used by the marine branch of the German Air Force; that is to say, it was of the pneumatic type, to be inflated when required. Such boats were standard equipment in all German sea-going aircraft. Evidently it had been required for some purpose, presumably to enable the sailors to get to and from the ship without using the gangway—or else to enable them to examine the far side of the ship from water-level. Biggles felt that if he could secure this useful craft without being observed it would serve his purpose admirably.

The fact that it was dark simplified his task; and that the sailors were too concerned with their respective duties to notice what others were doing, was another factor in his favour. So, taking every opportunity when the coast was clear, he worked his way along the beach, drawing ever closer to his objective, until at last he slipped quietly into the frail craft and pushed himself clear. Any noise that he made, and it was negligible, was drowned in the hammering that was still going on. Picking up the paddle, he worked his way round to the far side of the ship—that is, the side farthest from the shore, and from which, of course, he could not be seen from the beach. Here he felt comparatively safe, and he experienced that thrill of satisfaction which comes when a difficult job has been well begun.

The next step was to discover, if possible, the cabin in which Algy was confined. That it would be fitted with a porthole he felt sure, but even so there was no indication of the side of the ship it would be on. He had simply gone to the far side first because it presented less danger than the near side. If he could not locate Algy, then he would have to go aboard to seek him, trusting in his uniform, or the Gestapo pass, to carry him through if he were questioned.

He spent nearly half an hour working up and down the side of the vessel, trying each porthole in turn, peeping into those that were open and tapping on the glass of those which were not. But it was all in vain, and finally he was compelled reluctantly to conclude that Algy must be on the other side of the ship; either that or in a central hold unprovided with any direct communication with the outer air. It was clear that no further progress could be made unless he actually went on board the ship, and this he now determined to do. A rope ladder hung conveniently—too conveniently he afterwards realized—from the rail, and up this he now proceeded. As his eyes drew level with the deck he looked around. Not a soul was about. In a moment he had swung a leg over the bulwarks and was aboard. A ventilator offered a handy hiding-place, but he had not taken more than two paces towards it when a voice spoke.

'Welcome on board, Major Bigglesworth,' it said mockingly.

Biggles spun round. And that was all he could do, for menacing him from half a dozen places were as many weapons. He could not distinguish the features of the man who had spoken, but he recognized the voice only too well: it was that of von Stalhein.

The German stepped forward. 'We were expecting you,' he said suavely.

'And just why were you expecting me?' inquired Biggles.

Von Stalhein laughed softly. 'With Lacey here, a

169

prisoner, it was obviously only a question of time before you arrived.'

Biggles perceived the truth of this assertion, and bit his lip in vexation.

'I was so sure that you'd come,' continued von Stalhein pleasantly, 'that I arranged for a boat to be convenient, and for a rope ladder to enable you to get aboard. So you see, Major Bigglesworth, we can do a little planning—as well as you.'

'You've been so slow about it this time that I'd almost forgotten it,' rejoined Biggles smoothly. 'I'll be more careful on future occasions.'

'It is unlikely that there will be any future occasions,' said von Stalhein softly.

'I seem to have heard you say that before, too,' Biggles told him.

'Quite right,' admitted the German frankly, 'but we all learn from experience—or we should. As far as you are concerned, I'm afraid the opportunity has passed. Hitherto it has always been a source of irritation to me that at least one of you was at large, even although I held the other two; but at last, as was bound to happen sooner or later, I have you all in the net together. You cannot imagine the satisfaction that it gives me.'

Biggles did not understand. He knew, of course, that Algy was a prisoner, but von Stalhein spoke as if he held Ginger, too, and that, surely, was impossible. He suspected a trap, and was careful to be non-committal in his reply. 'Congratulations,' was all he said.

'Ah, I see there is a doubt in your mind,' continued von Stalhein imperturbably. 'A doubt about our young friend with the difficult name—Hebblethwaite. You

170

will be sorry to learn that he has had a piece of bad luck.'

'Really?' Biggles was still taking no chances of giving information away.

'Yes,' went on the other, fitting a cigarette into a long holder. 'He had the misfortune to fall into the sea, where he would certainly have drowned had it not been for the timely arrival of one of our submarines, which rescued him. The commander of the submarine that picked him up signalled to his base for instructions, so, naturally, as the boat was not far away, I asked for him to be brought here. Presently you will all be together, when you will be able to compare notes, and ascertain, perhaps, how and where your plan went wrong.'

Biggles did not know whether to believe him or not, but it was not like the German to lie over such a matter; there appeared to be no point in it; moreover, there was a ring of confidence in his voice that made the statement sound like the truth. Biggles realized that such a state of affairs as the one von Stalhein had described might easily have come to pass.

'You certainly seem to hold all the cards,' he conceded. 'What are you going to do about it?'

Von Stalhein ignored the question. 'How would you like to have a chat with Lacey?' he suggested.

'Thanks.'

'I am sorry Hebblethwaite is not here yet, but his arrival cannot be long delayed. When he comes I'll send him down to join you. I'm sure he will be overjoyed to see you again, even though, of course, the reunion will be for a short time only. I am very busy at the moment, as you will readily believe, but I can give you until the morning to write any messages that you may wish to send home. Colonel Raymond, for example, will doubtless be anxious to hear how it all came about—unless he is too overwhelmed by the disaster which by that time will have overtaken the British naval forces operating on the Norwegian coast. With your admirable knack of learning things, no doubt you have heard about the little surprise we have in store.'

'Mind your scheme doesn't go off in your hand and burn your fingers,' warned Biggles coolly. 'The ships aren't in the fiord yet.'

He spoke mockingly, but his heart was sick, for if what von Stalhein had said was indeed true, and there seemed little reason to doubt it, then he could not imagine how the fleet could escape.

Von Stalhein went on. 'After your recent feverish activities—carried out, I must confess, with your customary initiative and zeal—you must be weary. Come below and join Lacey. Oh, we'd better have that pistol of yours, if you don't mind.'

Biggles had no alternative but to hand over the weapon. To attempt to use it at this juncture would have been suicidal, for he was still covered by half a dozen weapons at point-blank range. Having handed it over, he proceeded with an escort down the companionway.

As he had already begun to suspect, the cabin in which Algy was confined turned out to be in the middle of the ship. Light was admitted during the day through a heavy glass skylight in the deck immediately overhead. An armed sentry was on duty outside the door.

Von Stalhein opened it and went in. The cabin was lighted by a single unprotected electric-light globe. 'A friend of yours to see you,' he said, with just a trace of cold humour in his voice.

Algy was sitting on a bunk, but he jumped up when he saw Biggles. 'Hello! I expected you'd be along,' he said cheerfully.

Von Stalhein screwed his monocle into his eye. 'This is a picture I've always wanted to see,' he remarked softly. 'Well, I shall have to leave you now. Make the most of your time. The fiord will be abandoned first thing in the morning, but as our accommodation is limited you will not be coming with us.'

'Quite so,' answered Biggles calmly.

'Your young friend will be joining you shortly,' promised von Stalhein, and went out.

The door was bolted on the outside, and the sentry resumed his pacing up and down.

Biggles seated himself on the bunk. 'So here we are,' he murmured.

'How did it happen?' asked Algy—referring, of course, to Biggles's capture.

'I was trying to get to you, but unfortunately von Stalhein anticipated the move and was waiting for me. I should have come anyway, of course.'

'I was afraid of that,' said Algy sadly. 'I suppose he told you about Ginger being captured?'

Biggles nodded.

'D'you think it's true?'

'I'm afraid it is. I don't see what purpose he could have in lying to us.'

'How did they get hold of him, I wonder?'

'We got together during the day,' explained Biggles. 'You saw me take off with Schaffer? As soon as we were in the air I grabbed the machine. Ginger was hanging about outside the fiord, and in trying to shoot us down got shot down himself. I picked him up, and then came ashore while he went off in the machine to look for the fleet. Presumably he was shot down, or ran out of petrol; anyway, he must have found himself on the water, and was picked up by a U-boat. It's this business of the fleet that upsets me more than anything.'

'He might have got through to it.'

Biggles shook his head. 'I doubt it. If he did, it's unlikely that he would have been captured.'

'He might have delivered the message and then started back to pick us up, hoping that we'd got away.'

'There's just a chance of that,' agreed Biggles, 'but somehow it doesn't strike me as being the answer. If he was picked up by a U-boat, then he must have been in the water, and had all been well he wouldn't have been in that position.'

Algy shook his head. 'I still think he might have been prowling about the coast looking for us, and ran into trouble.'

'It's no use guessing,' declared Biggles. 'No doubt he'll tell us how it happened when he arrives—not that it matters very much now. Von Stalhein has got us in a nasty jam, and it would be foolish to deny it. Still, it isn't the first time.'

'I gather from what he told me that he intends to—er—dispose of us in the morning.'

'That, I imagine, is his idea,' returned Biggles. 'But it isn't mine. Morning is a long way off. Let's have a look round to see if there's any way out of this den.'

'There isn't—I've looked,' returned Algy promptly.

'Jack Shepherd once asserted, and on more than one occasion proved, that neither bolts nor bars will hold a man if he is determined to get out. There's always a way—if you can find it. Let's try.'

They made a complete survey of the cabin, and were soon forced to admit that escape appeared to be a hopeless proposition. There were only two exits. One was the door, which was bolted and guarded by a sentry. The other was the skylight in the deck, which they had no means of reaching; in any case it seemed to be fastened from the outside. For the rest, a glance was enough to reveal the futility of trying to make any impression on the heavy, hard-wood timbers of which the ship was built. It would have been difficult enough with proper tools, and they had nothing remotely resembling a cutting instrument. Nor was there a fitment of any sort that could be removed and used as a weapon. There was a bunk at one end of the cabin, but like everything else it was stoutly built and offered no solution to the problem. There was a mattress in it, together with a rather dirty sheet and an old brown blanket. Biggles looked at them reflectively for a moment or two and then turned back to Algy.

'I agree with you in this respect,' he said. 'There's only one way out of this room, and that's the way we came in—through the door.'

'It's not likely to be opened.'

'On the contrary, it will be opened when Ginger arrives.'

'Yes, but he'll have an escort of at least two or three armed men with him. We're hardly in a case to take them on with our bare fists.'

'By the time they arrive we ought to have something better than bare fists,' asserted Biggles. 'After all, we have this advantage. We know that the worst that can happen is that we shall be shot, and as we shall be shot in any case if we don't get away, we've nothing to lose if we fail.'

'Really, they've absolutely no right to shoot us,' protested Algy.

'What von Stalhein has a right to do, and what he does, are two entirely different things,' returned Biggles smiling. 'If he needs an excuse for treating me as a spy, he's got one in this Boche uniform I'm wearing. But we're wasting time. I'm going to see about getting out.'

'What, now?'

'Certainly. There's only one sentry on duty. We'll tackle him first.'

Biggles took up a position immediately under the electric-light bulb. 'Switch off the light,' he ordered. 'I don't want to electrocute myself.'

Algy crossed to the switch and turned off the light. He heard the sound of a jump, followed by a splintering noise. 'What on earth are you doing?' he muttered.

'It's all right, I've got what I wanted,' answered Biggles. 'It's the electric flex.' As he spoke he removed the bulb from the end.

'What are you going to do with that wire?'

'I'll show you. What I want you to do now is lie here, just inside the door, and groan. When the sentry comes in he's bound to look at you—enough light will come in from the corridor for him to see you. I shall then proceed to throttle him with the noose I'm making in this flex. All right, go ahead with the groaning; I'm all ready, and we've no time to waste.'

Algy did as he was told, and his groans echoed pitifully in the little cabin. Biggles waited until he heard

176

the sentry's footsteps approaching and then hammered on the door.

The sentry stopped. 'What is it?' he demanded.

'My friend is ill—I think he's dying,' answered Biggles, and Algy's groans seemed to confirm his statement.

A key scraped in the lock and the German looked in, bayonet at the ready. It was obvious from his attitude that he was taking no risks. 'What's happened to the light?' he asked, glancing up.

'It went out,' replied Biggles vaguely.

The sentry looked at Biggles, who was standing in a passive, dejected attitude, and then took a pace nearer to Algy, who was curled up on the floor, still groaning. He leaned towards him. 'What's the matter with you?' he asked gruffly.

Biggles jumped like a cat, slipped the noose over the man's head, and in a single jerk pulled it taut round his bare throat, cutting short the cry that rose to his lips. The rifle clattered to the floor as instinctively he clutched with both hands at the wire which was throttling him.

'Shut the door,' snapped Biggles.

Algy jumped to the door and closed it.

Biggles forced the sentry to the floor. 'Keep still or I'll choke you,' he snarled. Then to Algy, 'Get that sheet. Tear it into strips and tie him while I hold him.'

The sentry made no resistance. Indeed, as he was already nearly dead, he was in no condition to do so.

'Buck up,' urged Biggles. 'I don't want to kill the wretched fellow.'

For a minute or two, after he had loosened the wire, he really thought he had killed him, for the man's eyes were projecting and his tongue hanging out. His body was limp. However, by applying artificial respiration they restored him, after which Biggles relieved him of his jacket and trousers. This done, he was securely bound and gagged, and lifted into the bunk. The blanket was spread over him.

'Why all this performance?' queried Algy. 'There's nothing to prevent us making a bolt for it, is there?'

'You seem to have forgotten Ginger,' Biggles reminded him. 'We can't go without him. From now on I'm the sentry. As he spoke Biggles threw off his officer's uniform and put on that of the soldier. 'You stay here and keep an eye on Fritz,' he ordered. 'I'm going outside.'

'I get it,' answered Algy, as Biggles picked up the rifle and went out into the corridor.

'All clear,' he whispered; then he locked the door and took up the sentry's duties.

It was clear that everything now depended upon Ginger's early arrival, for should this be delayed a dozen contingencies might arise to betray the plot. The sentry might be relieved; von Stalhein might come and recognition follow; the N.C.O. in charge of the guard might come along and perceive that the sentry was not the man he had posted. Still it did not occur to Biggles to leave the boat without Ginger. The minutes ticked by. All seemed quiet. The men who had been working outside had evidently been dismissed.

# Chapter 15
# The Last Round

It was a good half-hour before Biggles heard with satisfaction the sound that he had so anxiously awaited; it was the tramp of feet coming up the gangway. There was a challenge; it was answered; the footsteps came on again, now on the deck, towards the head of the companion-way. Biggles walked up and down past the cabin door.

A minute later there appeared at the end of the corridor a procession consisting of four persons. First came a naval officer, in oilskins, a belt on the outside carrying a revolver-holster. He was followed by two seamen, also in oilskins, carrying rifles. Between them, looking very forlorn, marched Ginger. He did not even glance up as the party came to a halt in front of the door where Biggles awaited it.

Biggles saluted, unlocked the door, and threw it wide open. The party went on inside. All eyes were on Algy, for enough light entered from the corridor for him to be seen. Biggles brought up the rear.

As soon as he was across the threshold he dropped the point of his bayonet until it was pointing at the officer's back. 'The first man who moves or makes a sound dies,' he said quietly, but distinctly.

Every head, including Ginger's, turned.

Biggles stood like a statue just inside the doorway. His eyes met those of the officer. 'One sound and it will be your last,' he said coldly. 'We're desperate men. Algy, take his revolver. Ginger, collect the rifles.'

None of the Germans made a sound, nor did they protest; they seemed stunned, which was hardly surprising. Such movements as they made were slow, and they were disarmed almost before they realized what was happening.

Biggles now came inside and closed the door. 'Take thier oilskins and caps, then tie them up,' he ordered. 'Use the rest of the sheet, and the flex.'

As soon as this had been done he took the blanket, cut it into three pieces with his bayonet, and tied them over the prisoners' heads. 'They'll do,' he said shortly. 'Let's go. We've no time to talk now, but there's one thing I must know.' He turned to Ginger. 'Did you get that message through to the fleet?'

Ginger started. He seemed to be in a dream. 'No, I didn't,' he confessed. 'I looked for it until I ran out of petrol, then—'

'Never mind the rest,' cut in Biggles. 'That's all I want to know. We've got to get that message through somehow. There's still time, but there's only one way. A hundred yards along the beach there's a Dornier flying-boat. We've got to get to it. If there's trouble on the way and I drop out, don't wait for me. Go on to the machine. One of us at least ought to reach it. The fleet must come first. Let's get into these oilskins and caps; in the dark we ought to pass for the escort returning ashore having delivered the prisoner. We'll try to bluff our way through. If that fails we shall have to fight.'

He put on the officer's oilskins and cap. As the others followed suit with the remaining garments he looked them over critically. 'You'll do,' he announced. 'Let's march off.'

With Biggles at the head, the little party marched along the corridor to the companion-way. A dozen steps took them to the deck. Biggles did not stop, but went straight on to the gangway where a guard stood on duty. The night was cloudy, with rain threatening, so it was not until he was almost within touching distance of the guard that he saw, just beyond, near the stern, in the dim glow of a partly obscured lamp, two other men. One he recognized instantly by his figure; it was von Stalhein. The other appeared to be the captain. Biggles distinctly heard von Stalhein say, 'I must go below now; I want a few words with this new prisoner.'

Biggles did not alter his pace. The man on duty stiffened to attention as he passed, but said nothing. They went on down the narrow gangway to the rocks, which were deserted. Here Biggles paused for a moment to get his bearings, and it was while they stood thus, in the silence, that he heard von Stalhein speak to the man at the head of the gangway.

Said he, in the harsh peremptory tones which German officers employ when addressing subordinates, 'Did somebody go ashore just then?'

'Yes, sir,' answered the man. 'It was the guard that brought the prisoner aboard.'

Von Stalhein uttered an exclamation of annoyance. 'I wanted to speak to that officer,' he snapped, presumably to the captain. Footsteps moved swiftly towards the companion-way.

'We've got to get a move on,' said Biggles softly. 'He's going below. In three minutes he'll discover that his birds have flown. We'll make for the aircraft. Keep close, and don't make any noise unless it becomes necessary.'

They walked quickly along the beach to the point where the air squadron was stationed. Biggles hoped that no sentry would have been posted actually on the beach, but in this he was disappointed. A figure loomed up in the darkness.

'Halt! Who goes there?' rapped out a voice.

A split second later, before Biggles could reply, there was a shout from the boat, now some seventy or eighty yards away. 'Stop those men!' roared a voice.

The sentry took a pace nearer. 'Who are you?' he asked suspiciously, for he had, of course, heard the shout.

'Here's my warrant,' answered Biggles casually, taking a pace nearer as though to show a pass. At the last moment he moved like lightning. Grabbing the sentry's rifle with his left hand, he brought the butt of his revolver down on his head.

The sentry collapsed like a wet blanket.

By this time there was a commotion on the boat; von Stalhein's voice, shrill with anger, could be heard above others.

'Run for it,' said Biggles tersely, and sprinted along the beach until he was opposite the Dornier, which was anchored a few yards out.

He discovered the reason why it was so close as soon as he plunged into the water, for the beach shelved quickly, and he was wet to the waist by the time he reached the cabin door. Without waiting to see how the others fared, he ran forward and hauled up the anchor. By the time this was done the others were aboard, the flying-boat rocking with the abruptness of their entry.

'Algy, you take the centre gun-turret,' he ordered curtly. 'If there's no machine-gun, use your rifle, but don't start shooting until we're rushed. Ginger, stand by me and watch the shore. Tell me what happens. Use your rifle when you have to.' With that Biggles dropped into the pilot's seat, switched on the petrol and ignition, and felt for the starter.

'There's a crowd coming along the beach; I can hear them, but I can't see them yet,' said Ginger in the manner of a radio commentator. 'I can hear von Stalhein telling people to rush the machine,' he went on. 'The flying personnel are turning out. They're manning the searchlight.'

'Keep them back,' ordered Biggles, and the starter whirred. But the engine was cold and nothing happened. He tried again. Still nothing happened.

Ginger's rifle spat, and the single report was followed by the crash of a machine gun somewhere close at hand. In the middle of the pandemonium that followed the engine came to life. Simultaneously several shots were fired at the machine. Ginger staggered back and flopped down, grabbing his shoulder. His rifle clattered to the floor. 'They've got me,' he muttered. 'Go on, it's only my shoulder.'

Algy's gun was playing a vicious tattoo on the crowd rushing towards the aircraft, but it was drowned in the roar of the engine as Biggles opened the throttle. The Dornier surged forward across the smooth surface of the fiord.

'We're away,' cried Ginger weakly, pressing his hand on his wound.

183

But Biggles was not so sure. He couldn't see a thing. To make matters worse, the searchlight suddenly came on, and the beam, sweeping low across the water, came to rest on the flying-boat, dazzling him. Actually, it was this light that gave him his position, for he knew where it was stationed. The difficulty was, it was only possible to take off straight down the centre of the fiord, and if he veered to either side he was likely to collide with the cliffs that hemmed it in. Knowing the position of the searchlight, he swung the aircraft round until it was facing what he thought—and hoped—was the right direction, and pushed the throttle wide open. He dared not delay any longer, for shots were now striking the machine, and he knew that it only needed one in a vital place to put it out of action.

Bending forward to peer through the windscreen into the blackness ahead, he held the joystick forward, and waited. The stick tightened as the machine gathered flying speed. He gave it another few seconds to be on the safe side and then took it off the water.

Algy's gun ceased firing and presently he appeared. 'Have a look at Ginger,' ordered Biggles. 'He's been hit. There ought to be a first-aid outfit on board.'

Algy disappeared into the cabin, and presently came back with the outfit. 'I've got it,' he called. 'Incidentally, I see we've got a load of bombs on board.'

'Have we though?' A curious smile crossed Biggles's face as he said the words. He looked down. Now at two thousand feet, just below the clouds, the coast-line and the outlines of the fiord could easily be traced. He could not actually see the boat from which they had just escaped, but he knew roughly where it was, and he swung round in a wide curve to fly back over it.

Two or three other searchlights had now joined the first, and their beams criss-crossed the sky in search of him. Flecks of flame showed where flak was bursting, but the fire was not intense and caused him little concern. A glance over his shoulder revealed Algy attending to Ginger. Then he went on with his eyes on the target. His hand moved to the bomb release and the load of high explosive went hurtling down, to burst with a glare that lit up the sky like lightning. It was, of course, impossible to ascertain what damage had been done, but satisfied with his parting shot, Biggles turned towards the west, and soon the coast was a dark shadow behind him.

He was now faced by two problems, although they were to a great extent linked together. The first was how to warn the fleet of its danger, and the second, how to get home in a German machine without being shot down by British anti-aircraft defences. He felt that if he could solve one, the other might solve itself. That is to say, if he could make contact with the fleet, or any British patrol vessel fitted with wireless, the warning would be flashed out, and they, at the same time, would be picked up. The trouble was, he had no idea of the position of the fleet. Thinking it over, he saw that an alternative would be to fly straight on home. It would come to the same thing in the end, for a radio message would soon stop the fleet. After some consideration he decided that an attempt to locate the fleet might end, as Ginger's flight had ended, in running out of petrol before the object was achieved; he resolved, therefore, to go straight on towards England. If he passed a patrol ship on the way, well and good.

He would try to land near it and get the skipper to send the all-important warning.

Algy, having got Ginger comfortable, joined Biggles in the cockpit.

'How is he?' asked Biggles.

'Not bad. The bullet got him just under the collarbone and went right through. He'll be all right after a day or two in hospital. How are we going to get on the carpet without being shot to bits by our own people?'

'I've just been thinking about the same thing,' answered Biggles. 'If there was a torch on board we could signal in Morse.'

Algy made a search, but came back to say that he couldn't find one. 'There are a couple of parachutes, some flares, and some parachute-flares,' he announced. 'If you can get over the coast I wouldn't mind going down on a parachute to arrange for a landing. I could at least stop the guns—'

'No use,' broke in Biggles. 'Apart from the risk of being shot down while crossing the coast, it would take too long.'

'Then how about landing on the water if it isn't too rough?' suggested Algy.

'And find ourselves in the middle of the main minefield? It runs right down the coast, you know. Not for me. Our best chance, I think, is to risk everything and go right on—unless we spot a ship on the way.'

'If we do it will shoot at us.'

'In that case we'll pretend to be hit and land on the water. Then we should be picked up. Let's have a look at the water for a start. Get ready to drop a parachute flare.'

Biggles took the Dornier down to a few hundred feet,

and in the light of a parachute-flare saw that the sea was comparatively calm; but it seemed that the flare was seen by other eyes, too, for almost at once, no great distance away, a searchlight stabbed the sky. Biggles didn't wait for the flak which he knew would follow. Blipping* his engine to attract attention, he went straight on down and landed on the water, where a few minutes later, the searchlight picked up the machine.

'We should look silly if that vessel turned out to be a Hun,' remarked Algy.

'The chances of a German ship being in the North Sea are so small that we needn't consider them,' Biggles told him confidently.

His confidence in the Navy keeping the sea clear of enemy shipping was justified a few minutes later when the slim outline of a British destroyer loomed up in the gloom. Naturally it carried no lights. The airmen were already hailing it, yelling that they were British, to prevent a mistake that might end in tragedy.

'Who are you?' came a voice, amplified by a mega-phone.

'British prisoners escaping in a German plane,' roared Biggles. 'Please pick us up.'

Further explanations at that stage were unnecessary, but the destroyer was taking no risks, and its guns were trained on the aircraft as it came alongside.

In five minutes the three friends were aboard her, talking to her commander in his cabin. Ginger, with his arm in a sling, looking rather pale, was present, for he had insisted on making light of his wound.

'My name's Bigglesworth,' announced Biggles with-

*Changing the rhythm and sound of the engine by closing and opening the throttle rapidly.

out preamble. 'I'm a Squadron Leader in the R.A.F. These are two of my officers. We've just come from Norway.'

The skipper started. 'Why, I've heard of you,' he declared. 'Aren't you the fellows who got the message through to the fleet, warning it to keep out of Westfiord?'

Biggles stared. 'Then the fleet's all right?'

'You bet it is.'

Biggles sank down in a chair and wiped imaginary perspiration from his brow. 'Phew! That's a relief,' he muttered. 'But how did it happen—I mean, how did the fleet get the message?'

'I don't know the details,' answered the captain. 'All I know is that one of our Intelligence blokes—a fellow named Bigglesworth, so it was said—got into touch with the skipper of a trawler. The skipper sent a signal to the Admiralty, and the Admiralty issued fresh orders to the fleet. That's all there was to it.'

'But the trawler was sunk by a torpedo,' burst out Ginger.

'That's right—but that happened afterwards. The skipper had already been in touch with the Admiralty. Shortly afterwards another signal came through from the same trawler, this time an SOS, to say that they had been torpedoed and were sinking. One of our destroyers hurried along and picked up most of the survivors. Apparently some time was spent looking for the fellow who had brought the message about the trap that had been laid for the fleet, but he couldn't be found.'

'For a very good reason,' put in Ginger, smiling. 'He had already been picked up by the U-boat. It was me.' He looked at Biggles. 'So that's how it happened.'

'That's it,' continued the skipper. 'I'll put you ashore as soon as I can. Meanwhile, is there anything you want?'

'Plenty,' returned Biggles promptly. 'Among other things a bath, a square meal, a comfortable bunk, and home.'

'If that's all, I think we can supply the lot,' grinned the naval officer. 'We're going back to port to refit—in fact, we're setting a course for home right now. Come below and I'll fix you up with the rest.'

'Lead on,' invited Biggles.

Five hours later, without misadventure, the destroyer steamed slowly into an east coast port. The comrades, washed and refreshed by a short sleep, watched the landing-jetty creep nearer.

'Do you see what I see?' murmured Ginger.

'I think so,' replied Biggles. 'You mean Colonel Raymond? I expected that he'd be here. I got the skipper to send a signal saying that we were aboard.'

As the destroyer was made fast Colonel Raymond came briskly across the gangway. 'Welcome home,' he said cheerfully. 'Between ourselves, I was just beginning to wonder if you ever would get home,' he confessed.

'You didn't wonder about that as much as we did, I'll warrant,' remarked Biggles grimly. 'If you've come here to say that something, somewhere, is waiting to be done, then I'll tell you right away that you've come to the wrong place.'

'Oh dear! I'm sorry to hear that,' announced the Colonel in a pained voice.

Biggles looked at him suspiciously. 'Then you *had* got something on your mind?'

'Yes. As a matter of fact, I had a little idea,' admitted the Colonel. 'I've got my car here, and I thought perhaps a bite of dinner at the Savoy—'

Biggles caught him by the arm. 'That's different,' he declared emphatically. 'If that's the next mission, let's get right along. When you hear what we've got to tell you I think you'll agree that we've earned it.'